LOVE lessons

D0524783

David Belbin

SCHOLASTIC
PRESS

For Julia

Scholastic Children's Books,
Commonwealth House, 1-19 New Oxford Street,
London WC1A 1NU, UK
a division of Scholastic Ltd
London ~ New York ~ Toronto ~ Sydney ~ Auckland

First published in the UK by Scholastic Ltd, 1998

Copyright © David Belbin, 1998

ISBN 0 590 54229 X

Typeset by DP Photosetting, Aylesbury, Bucks.
Printed by Cox and Wyman Ltd, Reading, Berks.

10 9 8 7 6 5 4 3 2 1

Part One

Prologue

It happened in October, two days before the half-term break. School was about to finish for the day and the English lesson was winding down. The teacher, Mr Scott, was the only one who Rachel really liked at Stonywood. He told stories and somehow had the trick of teaching you things without you realizing.

"Coming back to the mock exams ..."

Behind Rachel, Kate Duerden and Lisa Sharpe were discussing Mr Hansen, the new maths teacher.

"I caught him looking at me today," Kate whispered, dreamily.

"He's meant to look at you," Lisa said, sounding bored. "That's his job."

"He's not paid to look at me the way he looked at me today," Kate retorted. "You know what else he did? As I was leaving, he winked at me."

"Dream on," Lisa told her. "It was probably a facial twitch."

"Coming back to the mock exams ..." Mr Scott repeated, then saw where the noise was coming from. "If I could have your attention, ladies. There are two minutes of the lesson left and I have a little information of some value to impart ..."

Rachel liked the deliberately old-fashioned way he talked sometimes, taking the mickey out of himself. English was her best subject, the only class where she didn't spend half her time daydreaming. It was also the only class where she was in the same group as her best friend, Becky.

Mr Scott coughed, loudly. Rachel focused a serious face on him. Behind her, Kate stopped discussing the new maths teacher. Mr Scott, his face slightly red, said "Thank you," then took a deep breath. "Now then, as you know, the literature exam in December consists of three questions: one on the poetry anthology, one on the novel, and one on the play."

"But we haven't started the play yet!" complained Nick Cowan, who sat in the front row.

"Precisely," said Mr Scott, impatiently. "Which is why, in order to make the exam as realistic as possible ... as realistic..."

He paused, and took another breath. "In order to make the exam as realistic as possible, you will have to answer two questions on one text and ..."

He stopped again. His face, Rachel saw, had become very flushed. The class was silent. Becky, her voice embarrassed but concerned, called out, "Are you all right, sir?"

The teacher clearly wasn't all right. He clutched his chest and began to sway, falling against Nick Cowan's desk. The class watched in shocked silence as Mr Scott's limp body hit the floor.

Then there was pandemonium.

One

"What happened next?" Rachel's mum asked.

"Becky went over to him, loosened his tie and all that. I ran for the nurse. It was terrible. Just as I left the room, the bell went for the end of school, so I had to push my way through all these kids in the corridor. I was sure he'd be dead by the time I got back."

"And was he?"

Rachel shook her head. "When I got to the office, the nurse wasn't there. She was visiting a primary school or something. So the office called an ambulance and the Head ran back to the classroom with me. It was weird. Half the class had left and everybody else was just sitting there, looking petrified. Mr Scott was still unconscious on the floor. Becky said she thought he was still breathing. The Head told everyone to go, so we left. The ambulance arrived as we got out of school."

Rachel had been crying. Mum gave her another tissue.

"It sounds like you behaved very sensibly. I'll give Janet a ring in a few minutes, find out how Colin is. You go and lie down. You've had a shock. I'll come up and tell you as soon as I find anything out."

"OK."

Rachel hugged Mum, then went upstairs to her bedroom. Mum was one of the parent-governors at Stonywood Comp. That was why the Head was "Janet" and Mr Scott, "Colin".

Sometimes this embarrassed Rachel. Today, though, she was glad of it.

In the room, Rachel kicked off her shoes and got into bed, fully clothed. Then, too hot, she threw the duvet covers off and stared at the pale pink ceiling of her room. She had chosen the colour herself two years earlier. Then, it felt fresh and feminine. Now, she didn't like it. Sometimes she wished her room was painted black, like a cave. She wanted it to be a dark, secret place where she could hide from the world and be herself. But her room was pink.

Footsteps sounded on the stairs. Mum knocked on the door.

"I'm awake."

Mum came in, still wearing the grey skirt and matronly knitted top she'd gone to work in that morning. Mum was a secretary at a solicitor's. Thirty-six years of age, she looked older. Rachel blamed this on the fact that she'd spent the last ten years bringing up a child on her own. Mum sat on the edge of the bed. Her face told Rachel all she needed to know.

Mum held Rachel's hand. "Colin had a second heart attack on the way to the hospital, love. There was nothing they could do to save him."

Rachel hugged her mother. "Why?" she asked her. "Why?"

But, for the first time Rachel could remember, Mum had no answers.

Two

Rachel felt out of place at Mr Scott's funeral. She'd come with Mum, who was a friend of the teacher's wife. It was during half-term and she was the only kid there. That was, unless you counted the teacher's teenage children, silent as statues on the front row. But Rachel would have felt worse if she hadn't come. Mr Scott had taught her for three of the previous four years. He knew that Rachel wanted to act and, last year, got her an audition for the drama workshop run by Central TV. Rachel didn't get in, but she'd never have had the chance if it weren't for Colin Scott. Sometimes, Rachel had wished that the teacher were her father, rather than the slick, self-centred man she saw every other weekend.

"Sudden deaths are always the hardest to bear," said the vicar. "Colin Scott was taken from us in the prime of his life, depriving Lucy, Martin and Sally of a dearly beloved father and leaving Tina to face life without her devoted husband. He was a dedicated man – to his family, and to his job. Perhaps it can be said he worked harder than was good for him, never refusing tasks, no matter how big or small ..."

Across the aisle, Rachel thought she saw Ms Howard, the head of English, bristle. The eulogy moved on to the mysteriousness of God's ways. Rachel let the vicar's clichés wash over her. Minutes later, the casket slid silently behind a red, velvet curtain and Rachel burst into tears.

Outside, afterwards, Rachel was surprised to find that

Colin Scott had been forty-four, only five years older than her own father. She waited for Mum to drive her home. The sun was brighter than it had any cause to be. Leaves on the trees were turning from brown to gold, then falling softly on to the ground. This was the first time that someone close to Rachel had died. She didn't know how to deal with it.

Rachel went over to see if she could hurry Mum up. She was talking to Ms Howard, a stuffy, ambitious woman who Rachel didn't like. The vicar had been right about Mr Scott being pushed too hard. Rachel had seen the way Ms Howard acted during the school play last year, getting him to do most of the work while she took most of the credit. Now, she was embarrassed to hear Mum say, "I know this isn't really the place to ask, but I'm worried about Rachel's English. It's her best subject and, with Colin gone, will you be able to take over the group?"

"I'm afraid not," Ms Howard said. "I have a top group in the other half year. The timetables clash."

Rachel was relieved to hear that.

"But we're hoping to get someone in quickly. In fact, Janet Perry and I are interviewing a young man tomorrow. Just out of a teacher training course, but he's got a first class honours degree."

"Sounds promising," Mum said, then noticed her daughter listening.

"Can we go?" Rachel asked, tersely.

The two women broke apart guiltily, like schoolgirls caught talking in class. It was sick, Rachel thought. Mr Scott had been dead less than a week, and they were already appointing his replacement. Whatever he was like, Rachel knew that she would hate him.

Three

Mike woke early, the way he always did when he had an interview. He stared at the ceiling for an age, running over questions in his mind. At seven, he got out of bed quietly, in order not to wake Emma. His girlfriend was still a student, in the second year at Hallam University, and didn't have a lecture until ten. Emma was lending him the car, which her parents had bought her when she passed her A-levels. Mike showered and trimmed his beard. He'd grown the beard for teaching practice to make him look older, more authoritative. It was a pain to keep up, but Emma thought it was cute, so the beard stayed.

Mike shovelled down some cornflakes, then borrowed Emma's new tape to play on the journey. He stepped over a crumpled NME, Emma's Doc Marten's and two pairs of torn jeans to get back to the bed. His girlfriend was still sleeping, her fine brown hair falling over the duvet. Mike kissed her neck, then left the flat quietly.

Fifty minutes later he was in Nottingham. Stonywood was just off the ringroad, not far from the city centre. Mike got out and looked around. It was a crisp autumn day. Pale brown leaves drifted from a solitary tree on to the almost empty car park. Cotton-wool clouds floated across a paintbox blue sky. In its brochure, Stonywood school sounded super-modern – all information technology and courses geared to the individual student. Up close, its mix of redbrick and prefabricated buildings resembled nothing more than Mike's teaching practice school in Sheffield. He felt comfortable.

Jobs were tight this year. You'd have thought that, with a good degree and teaching qualification, he'd walk into one. But Mike had a shy side and often froze in interviews. He'd blown his last one in Worksop the week before. When the Head called him back afterwards, Mike assumed that he was going to be given the usual, useless pep talk. Instead, he was told about Stonywood, whose Headteacher had rung that afternoon, asking whether there was a good candidate left over from the interviews. They had a sudden vacancy.

Mike had been applying for jobs within commuting distance of Sheffield, because of Emma. He'd only been applying for jobs at 11-18 schools, because he wanted sixth-form teaching. Stonywood had no sixth form. But a job was a job. Mike consulted Emma. To his surprise, she encouraged him to apply. Emma was fond of Sheffield, but, like Mike, was from Leicester. Nottingham was nearer home. Also, it was meant to be an exciting city to live in. If Mike got the job, they could move there after Emma finished her degree. But that was a long way off.

Judith Howard showed him round. Parts of the school were shiny new, like its glossy brochure. The English rooms, however, were rather shabby. The displays were old-fashioned, and didn't seem to have been changed recently. It looked like they needed some new blood. Mike did his best to ask intelligent questions. The head of English seemed suitably impressed.

The Headteacher was a well-dressed, grey-haired woman in her late forties. "It's a temporary contract," Mrs Perry said, after a few, perfunctory questions, "for two-and-a-half terms. It's too early to say if the contract will be renewable. Mr Scott had a year-eleven exam class, which is why we're eager to appoint quickly. If we went through the usual channels, they wouldn't have a teacher until January at the earliest. So, the question is, can you start on Monday?"

Mike blinked. He couldn't believe that, after six months and seventeen interviews, someone was finally offering him a job. "Er, yes, fine," he said, in an off-hand voice.

The Head reached over and shook his hand. The contract, he realized, was sealed.

The next hour, when Judith Howard went over the timetable with him, passed in a daze. It was only when he was walking back to the car, with an armload of policy documents, textbooks and class readers, that Mike began to wonder what he was letting himself in for. But the doubts passed quickly. He stopped at an off licence on the way home to buy a bottle of sparkling wine.

"That's brilliant!" Emma said, hugging him.

"I thought we'd get a takeaway to celebrate," Mike said.

Emma smiled, then pulled off his tie and began to undo the buttons of his shirt. "Forget the takeaway for now. Bring two glasses to the bedroom. I know a much better way to celebrate."

The new English teacher was tall and thin, with straight brown hair and a close-cut beard like Rachel's dad used to wear. Rachel hated beards. Mr Steadman's voice kept rising in an unnatural way – he was nervous, Rachel supposed – and he kept repeating everybody's names in a desperate attempt to memorize them. He also made weak jokes.

"So, the, er, poetry anthology you've been using is the, er,

Language of Love. Not something I've come across before."
Pause. "The book, I mean." No one laughed.

"I'll bet he's a virgin," Lisa Sharpe whispered, a row
behind Rachel.

Rachel grimaced. She didn't like to think of teachers
having sex lives. She felt sorry for this one. Some of the kids
in the school would eat him alive. But this was a top group
and – though few of the students would admit it – they were
anxious to pass their exams. The class would give this Mr
Steadman the benefit of the doubt. When he asked questions about what poems they'd already studied, people
answered politely.

"And which did you like best?"

There was the first of many awkward silences. Rachel,
who usually spoke a lot in English, remained silent. English
lessons often relied on people joining in discussion. If
Steadman wanted her contribution, he would have to earn
it, the way Mr Scott had done.

Rachel walked over to maths on her own. Becky was in a
top group for maths, while Rachel was in a middle one. As
she crossed the quad, Nick Cowan fell into step alongside
her. Rachel quite liked Nick, though he could be a bit – what
was the word? – *earnest* at times. He was in the same group
as her for maths, as well as English.

"What did you think of Steadman?" he asked.

"Not a lot," Rachel replied.

"He seems a bit wet behind the ears," Nick said.

It was the sort of expression Rachel would've expected
from her mother, not a sixteen-year-old boy.

"Still," Nick went on, "Scotty's a hard act to follow, isn't
he? You have to feel a bit sorry for him."

"I guess," Rachel muttered.

In maths, Rachel usually sat with Carmen, whom she'd known since primary school. Carmen was off school today, so Rachel pointedly sat at a table where there was only one seat left. She had the feeling that Nick was meaning to ask her something else. Now he was forced to sit across the room, on his own.

Mr Hansen came in. He was a slim, gentle-looking man with blond hair and blue eyes. Rachel could see why half the girls in her year fancied him. She wasn't one of them. Rachel was embarrassed when girls like Lisa and Kate made eyes at the teacher. They were so obvious that, at first, the teacher didn't know how to deal with them. Once he'd even blushed. He was used to it by now, though, and so should they be. Yet there was Lisa Sharpe, following him to the maths storeroom.

"Let me help you, sir."

"It's quite all right," Hansen said, in his soft, Scottish accent.

What did Lisa think, that Hansen would suddenly succumb to temptation and ravish her while twenty-eight students waited for tracing paper and calculators?

Hansen got the class to work in pairs. Rachel was sat at a table with four other people on it. Her usual partner being absent, she meant to work on her own, but the teacher wouldn't let her get away with it.

"Nick hasn't got a partner," he said. "Join him, would you?"

Rachel thought about protesting, but couldn't be so rude. Only immature girls like Lisa and Marie refused to work with boys.

Nick was better than her at maths. They got the work done in next to no time. That meant he got the chance to ask her the question she'd avoided earlier.

"Are you doing anything on Saturday night?"

"I…" Never any good at lying, Rachel didn't manage a reply.

"I haven't got it wrong, have I?" Nick stammered. "You aren't going out with anyone at the moment, are you?"

"No," Rachel admitted. "I'm not."

She looked at Nick. He had thick, dark hair, deep eyes and a strong chin. If Rachel didn't know him, she might find the boy attractive.

But she did know him. She'd seen him around the school since she was eleven years old and had shared two classes with him for a year and a bit. She knew that he stammered when he was nervous, had once been bullied by Bez McCloud and had a crush on Becky back at the beginning of year ten. Nick used to be cheeky to teachers but since his voice broke, giving him a deep growl, he had become more serious. He could also, Rachel knew, be very persistent. Like now.

"I was thinking we could go into town," Nick said. "See a film. You can choose. No pressure."

Rachel looked away. She wasn't doing anything on Saturday, and it was now too late to pretend that she was. She ought to explain to Nick that she liked him, but thought of him more as a brother than a potential boyfriend. However, if she said that, he would probably be insulted. Rachel didn't have a brother, not a proper one. How would she know what a brother was like? And she did like Nick. Kind of. It was just that she'd never thought of him the way he seemed to be thinking of her.

Until now. "OK," she heard herself saying.

Nick gave her a broad smile. "Brilliant," he said.

Four

"You're going out with Nick Cowan!" Becky repeated, as she and Rachel walked home together. "Why?"

"Because he asked me. Because I couldn't think of a reason to say 'no'. Because I didn't want to hurt his feelings. Anyway," Rachel added, "I like Nick."

"I see," Becky teased. "So why didn't you suggest that I go out with him when he asked me last year?"

"Nick's nicer than he was last year," Rachel argued. "You know it takes a while for boys to grow up." How did she find herself in this position, defending Nick Cowan? It wasn't as if she was serious about him.

"But he's not as nice as Carl, is he?"

"Carl's not around any more." Carl was Rachel's first and – so far – only serious boyfriend. She went out with him for four months, beginning in the middle of April and finishing in August, three months ago. He was in the year above her, a tall boy with long black hair and an infectious smile. He was shy, too, though not so shy that he hadn't asked Rachel to dance at a disco in the Easter holidays, then cycled round to her house the next day when Mum was out at work. He'd spent the rest of the Easter break round at Rachel's house, when he should have been revising.

Before Carl, Rachel felt like she knew nothing about life, especially boys. For ten days, the relationship was the most exciting thing that had ever happened to her. But then

Rachel was back at school. When Carl went on study leave, he wanted Rachel to skive off and spend time with him, but Rachel refused. Carl said that she was too straight. He thought it had something to do with her not being ready to have sex. But it wasn't only that. For one thing, Rachel didn't want to be blamed for Carl mucking up his exams.

The other thing was that she and Carl had less in common than she first thought. He loved music, and had introduced her to lots of groups who she still liked. But you couldn't sit and listen to music all the time. When they weren't kissing and cuddling, she and Carl struggled to make conversation.

Carl messed up his exams anyway. In the summer, his relationship with Rachel fizzled out. They went on holidays which didn't overlap. Rachel sent him a postcard, but never get one in return. When both were back in town, neither called the other. The next thing she knew, Carl was going out with some girl at the sixth-form college where he was retaking his GCSEs.

"I saw Carl in town on Saturday," Becky said. So that was why she'd mentioned him. Becky had always liked Carl. "He was asking after you. I think he's still interested."

"Well, I'm not interested in him," Rachel replied, tartly. Instantly, she wondered whether she meant what she'd just said. After all, if Nick could mature, so could Carl.

"No. You're more interested in Nick," Becky said.

"Leave it out, will you?" Rachel told her. "I said I'd go out with Nick once, that's all. He's not my boyfriend."

"Yet," Becky added, stopping at her gate. "Coming in?"

Rachel shook her head. "See you tomorrow."

"Hey, come on, can't you take a little teasing?" Becky said. "Nick's nice. He might be right for you, in a year or two."

Rachel gave her friend a playful punch, then walked the

rest of the way home alone. Becky could get away with being blasé about boys. She'd been going out with Gary for six months now. He was eighteen and worked at a travel agent's. They'd been sleeping together since early summer. Back then, Becky, Carmen and Rachel all had boyfriends, but now only Becky did. And only Becky had lost her virginity. Rachel and Carmen weren't ready, not yet.

"You must be in love with him," Rachel said at the time.

"We don't use the word *love*," Becky told her. "That's for magazines and pop songs."

Rachel wished that she was in a position to be so cynical. It hurt that the three of them weren't as close as they once were. She'd known Carmen longest but, since they wound up in the same form at secondary school, Becky had been her best friend. Rachel would give anything to have a really good relationship like Becky's. OK, Nick probably wasn't it. But there was no need for Becky to rub it in.

After school, Mike sat down next to the drinks vending machine in the empty staffroom, shattered. He didn't even have the energy to get a coffee. He'd been teaching for three days and wasn't sure that he would last until the weekend. A guy Mike's age wandered in, checked his pigeonhole, and looked around. He was a pale, thin bloke with a mop of blond hair. Seeing Mike, he smiled and walked over to the drinks machine. He pointed at it.

"You look knackered. Want a coffee?"

"Thanks. Black. No sugar."

The guy got two drinks and sat down next to Mike. When Mike fumbled in his pocket for change, he shook his head. "Forget it. I'm Phil Hansen, the other new bod. Maths."

"Mike Steadman." He shook Phil's hand. "English."

17

"How's it going?"

"All right. But I hadn't realized how exhausting it is."

"That's the way it goes," Phil said. "I can't believe how much work there is. I take an hour off, then work until ten most nights. Where're you living?"

"Sheffield."

"Sheffield?" Phil repeated, as though he hadn't heard right. "That's an hour's drive away."

"More at rush hour." Mike ought to get off soon, but didn't say so. Phil scratched his chin.

"Are you looking for a place round here?"

"Not really," Mike told him. "I share a flat in Sheffield. My girlfriend's still at university, and my contract's only temporary. I'm using her car at the moment, but I'm going to buy myself a banger at the weekend." That was, presuming the bank manager would increase his overdraft.

"It's a lot of travelling," Phil said. "I couldn't hack it. If you ever want a bed for the night, there's a spare one at my place."

"Thanks," Mike said, gratefully. "I might take you up on that." He looked at his watch. "If I don't go soon I'm going to run into a lot of traffic."

As he was getting into the car, a pretty girl from his year-eleven group came out of the music room, Becky something. She had a blonde bob and a swimsuit figure. Becky waved at him. He waved back, thinking that he must ask Phil Hansen what technique he used to learn names. There was a girl who sat next to Becky, just as good-looking but in a more subdued way. She hadn't spoken in their two lessons so far. What was she called? Mike didn't have the slightest idea.

Five

Rachel's father deserted her mum when Rachel was five years old. She was meant to spend every other weekend with him. However, he sometimes had to cancel and she hadn't seen him for over a month. Dad's house was twice the size of the one Rachel shared with Mum. Clarissa kept it surprisingly tidy, considering that there were two young children underfoot all the time.

Rachel loved Phoebe and Rowan, but had always kept her distance from Clarissa. She'd refused to go to the wedding. It took until she was ten before Rachel finally accepted that her parents would never get back together.

Rachel played with her half-brother and sister until it was time for dinner. The kids ate first, then there was a sit down meal with wine.

"Phoebe and Rowan are pleased to see you," Dad said, when he and Rachel were alone at the table. "Will you spend the evening with them?"

"Can't," Rachel said. "I'm going to a film with a friend."

Being at Dad's didn't stop Rachel going out on Saturday night if she wanted. In fact, Rachel was glad that she was going out. Sometimes, when she had nothing better to do, Dad expected her to babysit Phoebe and Rowan while he and Clarissa went to the pub. Rachel didn't mind doing babysitting when people paid her, which Dad and Clarissa did, on occasion. But she hated being exploited.

"Your friend," Dad said, as Clarissa brought in beef *en croute*, "is it anyone I know?"

"No," Rachel said. "It's just a boy from school. Nick."

That shut Dad up. Clarissa served the beef. It was very good. Dad and Clarissa always had the best of everything. Clarissa came from a family with money, which had paid for this house. She'd never needed to work.

"This boy," Dad said, as they were finishing. "Are you meeting him there?"

"No. He's calling for me."

Dad lived in Mapperley Park, which was nearer town than Stonywood. Nick had insisted on picking her up, splitting his journey.

"Good." Dad poured Rachel a glass of wine. "I've not met any of your boyfriends before."

"He's not my boyfriend," Rachel protested. "This is just a boy from school I'm going to the pictures with."

Dad turned to his wife.

"Did you use to draw that kind of distinction, Clarry?"

Clarissa gave her irritating, *I use to have a life, too* smile. "It depended who I was telling."

The doorbell rang.

"He's early," Rachel said. "I'll let him in."

Dinner was running late, so she should have known Nick would be early. He stood at the door, rain pouring on to his new-looking, black leather jacket.

"Hi, Rachel," he said. "You look nice."

"Thanks," Rachel said, adding courteously, "smart jacket."

"Sixteenth birthday present. Last week."

"You'd better come in."

"Bring him in here," Dad called from the dining room.

They hadn't had dessert yet, but Rachel never ate pudding here, telling Clarissa that she was watching her figure. Actually, nothing made Rachel put on weight. At home, she and Mum regularly pigged out on chocolate.

"Are you going to finish this, Rachel?" Clarissa asked.

There was still a potato on Rachel's plate.

"No. I've had enough. This is Nick. I'll only be a minute."

Rachel put her coat on. Back in the dining room, she found Nick deep in conversation with her father.

"Would you like to borrow my umbrella, Rachel?" Clarissa asked. "You don't want your coat to spoil."

"Thank you," Rachel said, brusquely.

Nick took the umbrella and held it over Rachel as they walked to the bus stop.

"Sorry to dump you with them," Rachel said, as they walked down the hill.

"It was fine," Nick said. "We talked about football. Eric gave me a glass of wine. Your mum seems nice."

Didn't Nick know anything? Couldn't he see that Clarissa was too young to have a daughter Rachel's age?

"She's not my mum," Rachel said, sharply. "She's Dad's second wife."

Nick looked embarrassed. He mumbled an apology.

"I wondered why you lived here, but went to Stonywood."

"It's all right," Rachel said, not wanting the evening to start on the wrong note. "You weren't to know."

They got into town early and walked up Chapel Bar to see what films were on. The city streets were busy, with more people flooding into the city on every bus.

"What do you fancy?" Nick asked.

There were nine films to choose from. The one Rachel

most fancied seeing was *When A Man Loves A Woman*. But the title might give Nick the wrong idea.

"How about *Pulp Fiction*?" she suggested. "I haven't seen it yet. Have you?"

"No," Nick said. "That's a good idea."

They were early so the queue was short.

"I'll pay for myself," Rachel insisted, as Nick fumbled in his pockets.

"Oh. Fine."

She bought her ticket at one counter, while Nick asked for his at the other.

"Are you eighteen, son?" the middle-aged woman asked him.

"Yes, of course."

Rachel, ticket in hand, froze with anticipated embarrassment.

"Got any ID?"

"Not on me, no."

The people in the queue behind Nick watched with amused curiosity.

"I'll check with the manager."

The woman waved at the manager. He took one look at Nick and shook his head.

"Sorry, duck. Do you want to see something else instead?"

Nick turned to Rachel, eyes pleading with her. She took over.

"We'll go and see *True Lies* instead. You'd better change this ticket for me, please."

They had half an hour to wait before the film began. At the bar, a young man served Nick two halves of lager without question.

"Sorry about that," he said. "I usually get away with it."

"I should have bought both tickets," Rachel said. "Girls look older. It's nothing to be ashamed of."

"You look about twenty," Nick said.

"Don't be daft."

"No, you do. I mean, even in school, you look ... you know, grown up. But, now, if I didn't know you, I'd never guess that you were only sixteen."

"Fifteen," Rachel said. "I'm not sixteen until April. And keep your voice down."

"Sorry. What are we going to see, anyway?"

"*True Lies.* Is that all right?"

She looked at his face. He was trying to decide whether to tell her something.

"You've seen it before, haven't you?"

"It's all right," Nick said. "I don't mind seeing it again. It's good fun."

Nick was right. The film was silly, but it took Rachel out of herself. She never normally went to see big screen blockbusters. It made her forget her nervousness about the date. Afterwards, they took the bus home. Nick offered to escort Rachel to her door, but she insisted that she would be safe walking up Tavistock Drive alone. If Nick walked her home he wouldn't get the last bus back to Stonywood. She would have to invite him in. Rachel wasn't ready to go that far.

"I had a nice time," Nick said, as the bus passed Clarendon College.

"Me too."

She rang the bell. The "Bus Stopping" sign lit up.

"Maybe we can do it again some time?"

"Yes," Rachel said. "Thanks for asking me."

She stood, and he sort of half stood, too. There was an

awkward pause, and Rachel thought for a moment that he was going to try and kiss her. But then he bottled it.

"See you on Monday," Rachel said. "Bye."

"Bye."

The road back up to Dad's house was dark and quiet. Although the area where Dad lived was leafy and expensive, the lower part was run down, all bedsits and student houses. Rachel worried about someone jumping out of the shadows, dragging her into one of the narrow passages which led down the sides. She walked quickly, keeping to the edge of the road, wishing that she had let Nick walk her home. She realized that she wouldn't mind going out with him again.

That was, if he asked her.

Six

On a grey Sunday afternoon in Sheffield, Emma ironed Mike's shirts for him.

"Is it always going to be like this?" she asked, as Mike sat at the kitchen table, preparing a sequence of year-eleven lessons for his second week at Stonywood. Before he got this job, they used to spend Sunday morning in bed, the afternoon with friends, and the evening in the pub.

"I expect it gets easier after a year or two," Mike replied.

Emma laughed. She thought he was joking. Yet, according to Phil Hansen, the more term went on, the more work built up. People went on about marking, but at least that was finite. Preparing lessons took the most time. He had to come up with five new ones every day, and, if they were no good, the kids played him up and he really suffered. What he'd said was true. When he'd been doing it for a year, it might get easier, because he'd have a stock of tried-and-tested lessons. But the end of the school year seemed an eternity away.

When Mike tried to explain this to Emma, she wasn't interested. Mike was meant to have found a car yesterday, but had been too tired to do anything about it. Emma was getting fed up with having to rely on the tram system to get to the university. There was something which he'd been putting off. Now seemed as good a time as any to tell her.

"I'm staying at Phil's on Thursday," Mike told Emma.

"There's a year-seven parents' evening. I won't finish until late."

"Thursday!" Emma protested. "You can't. We're going to see Sugar at the Foundry. Surely you could get home in time?"

Mike had forgotten the gig, the big reopening night of a local venue.

"I'll be too knackered to drive afterwards. Can you sell my ticket?"

"And go with who?" Emma moaned. "I was really looking forward to it."

"I'll make it up to you," Mike promised. "I'll buy us both tickets for the Oasis gig at the Arena."

At least, now that Mike had a job, he could afford to buy tickets for big shows.

"That's not until Easter," Emma complained.

"I'm really sorry," Mike said. "But it's my first parents' evening. I doubt that I'd be safe to drive home, never mind enjoy a gig." He gave her one of his sheepish smiles and Emma melted a little.

"I'll see if Carol wants to go to Sugar," she said, begrudgingly.

"Thanks."

She kissed him and, despite the work piled on the kitchen table, Mike was tempted to take things further. But then the phone rang.

"Steve!" Emma answered, cheerfully. "It's been ages. How are you?"

Mike went back to his lesson plans.

Steve was Emma's older brother, and used to be Mike's best friend. They'd nearly ended up going to the same university, only Steve didn't get as good grades as Mike. But then, the Christmas after their first term away, things went wrong.

Steve had a party and several of Emma's friends came. Mike had known Emma since she was eight. She was perky and pretty and just as intelligent as her brother. At one point, when she was thirteen, Mike had been vaguely aware that she had a bit of a crush on him. But he was sixteen, and she was just a kid then.

That New Year's Eve, Mike got chucked by Vicky, the girl he'd been going out with for the past eighteen months. He got blind drunk and ended up being comforted by Emma, now fifteen and no longer a kid. Not a lot happened, but enough for Mike to realize that Emma was seriously interested in him.

Mike's best friend warned him off. Steve was sympathetic about Vicky. But Emma was Steve's younger sister. Mike, an only child, could only imagine the way Steve felt. When Steve said, "She's too young for you, mate," Mike agreed. He tried to keep things cool. He tried to act like their kisses and hugs and heart-to-heart hadn't happened. But he kept going round to see Steve, and couldn't help seeing Emma, too. After a while, he began going home for the weekend when Steve wasn't around, but Emma was.

Emma started writing to him. Mike went out with women at university, but none of them set off sparks the way Emma did. In the long summer holiday, while Steve was working on a building site, Mike spent more and more time with his sister. They first slept together the night she got her GCSE results. By September, they were officially a couple.

Emma's parents took it better than Steve did. They liked Mike and trusted him. After six months, with Emma now seventeen and in the sixth form, they even sanctioned their daughter's occasional visits to Oxford. But Steve went ballistic. He and Mike never argued about it. They just stopped talking.

Another year passed. Emma got accepted by Sheffield and Mike arranged to do his PGCE there. They looked for a flat together. All this time, Mike hoped that his friendship with Steve would revive. It never had.

"How is he?" Mike asked, when Emma put the phone down.

"Fine. He wants you to get him two tickets for the Oasis concert."

"OK."

A chink of light, Mike thought. They hadn't been to a concert together in four years.

In bed that night, Mike was exhausted, but couldn't sleep. His mind kept going over his lessons for the year-eleven group. Last week they'd given him an easy time. But he was new, and their regular teacher had just died. The trouble was, he had few ideas about how to teach modern poetry. However, they were halfway through the book. It was too late to change text now. Mike found it difficult, standing up every other day and talking about love.

It worried him how often he found himself standing in front of a class, hardly knowing the first thing about the subject he was supposed to be teaching. Why should the kids listen to him? How long would it take before they found him out?

Seven

At the end of maths on Thursday, Nick gave Rachel a big smile. He wanted to talk, Rachel guessed, maybe ask her out again. But she left the room with Carmen, as usual.

"He's very friendly all of a sudden," Carmen said.

Rachel thought for a moment. Becky was sniffy about Nick and hadn't asked a lot about the date. Rachel had to talk about him with someone.

"I went out with him last Saturday night."

The words slipped out quietly, but Carmen's reaction was loud. "You're going out with *Nick*? I don't believe you!"

"No need to broadcast it to the world."

If a girl in Rachel's year had a boyfriend, he tended to be older than she was. Girls who went out with guys from the same year were looked down on by other girls. Everyone knew how immature the boys in their year were, had always been. But at least Carmen didn't get judgemental on her, the way Becky had.

"What was it like?" she asked, in a quieter voice.

"Fine. Except ..."

Rachel told Carmen the story about Nick not passing as eighteen.

"And are you seeing him again?"

"I've seen him in the last two lessons."

"You know what I mean."

Rachel answered reluctantly. "Maybe. I don't know." She

and Nick had hardly spoken since Saturday, which felt strange. "If he wasn't at school," Rachel added, "things'd be easier."

"If he wasn't at school," Carmen told her, "you wouldn't know him."

"Becky thinks I'm mad."

"Becky takes boys' attention for granted," Carmen said. "Nick's nice enough. Hey, look, I need to get in the lunch queue."

"OK. Don't tell anyone, huh?"

"Would I do a thing like that?"

Rachel went off to the common room. She didn't have a school lunch. The school meals were all pizza, burgers and chips, unless you got there in the first five minutes. Then there were a few tired, taste-free salads which were usually snapped up by teachers. It was simpler to bring your own food in. Rachel and Mum took turns to make a packed lunch each night. Rachel usually ate hers with Becky. However, on Thursdays, Becky had a music lesson. Rachel was about to get her sandwich box out when Nick walked into the common room. He smiled at her.

"On your own?"

She nodded. "Eat your lunch with me," Rachel invited. "If you like."

"People will talk."

"Let them," Rachel said, throwing caution to the winds. Why shouldn't she spend time with Nick if she wanted to?

"Actually," Nick said, "I haven't brought a packed lunch today. I only live down the road, so I was going to go home. Mum and Dad are both at work. Want to come with me?"

"Sure," Rachel said. "Why not?"

Nick's house was a semi, halfway up a hill beyond the

school. It was bigger than the terrace which Rachel shared with Mum, but much smaller than Dad's house.

Nick made a sandwich, then they went up to his room.

"It's a bit of a mess," Nick warned.

His room turned out to be tidier than Rachel's ever was. A few cassettes were scattered across the floor. He put one on. Rachel wasn't keen on it, but said nothing. Music wasn't everything. She and Nick sat at opposite ends of Nick's bed. Rachel was surprised by how many books Nick had, and commented on them.

"They're mostly science fiction," he said. "I use them to relax with, that's all. What do you read to relax?"

Rachel mainly read romances and women's magazines, but didn't want to admit it. So she fibbed.

"Poetry," she said, "and, you know ... magazines."

"I like poetry, too," Nick told her.

"The book we're doing in English is all right," Rachel said, tentatively.

"Yeah," Nick said, grudgingly. "I quite like it."

"What are your favourite bits?" Rachel asked, as she tried to eat her sandwich without getting crumbs all over Nick's bed.

"I like Norman MacCaig," Nick told her.

"I don't remember that one."

He went to his bag. For a moment, she thought he was going to read it to her, but he held the book open at the appropriate page instead. Rachel read the poem, "True Ways of Knowing", twice to make sure she understood it.

"That's lovely," Rachel said, putting the book down.

"Yeah. I like Shakespeare, too. The sonnet especially. What about you?"

"I like that poem, 'Actress'," Rachel said. "I want to be an actress."

"Really? I saw you in the school play last term. You were good."

"Thanks," Rachel said, flattered. "Mr Scott got me an audition with the Central Drama Workshop. I didn't make it, but I got on the reserve list."

"That's a pity," Nick said. "I used to go to the Central Workshop. We could have gone together."

Rachel was impressed. "You kept that quiet."

"We put on a play in Edinburgh last August," Nick said. "It was good fun. But I decided to give it a bit of a rest this year. Concentrate on exams."

"Actors don't need great exam results," Rachel insisted.

Nick shrugged modestly. "Maybe not, but I'd like to go to university. When I've finished that I can decide whether I want to act or not. Best to have something in reserve."

"I guess so," Rachel said.

She never worked terribly hard at school. It was easy to coast by. But Nick had a point. Until today, she'd found his keenness irritating. Now Rachel was seeing a new side to him. Maybe acting was what had made him mature over the last year.

The young couple moved closer to each other on the bed. When Nick asked Rachel to choose a tape, his body brushed against hers. She would have liked it if he hadn't moved away again. But they kept their distance. Lunch hour was quickly over.

As they were walking back to school, Nick asked, "Are you doing anything this Saturday night?"

"Nothing important."

He slipped his hand into hers. She let it stay there until they were within sight of the school gates.

Eight

After school on Friday, Judith Howard kept Mike behind for a mentor meeting. He could have done without it. A mentor was meant to be supportive; an experienced friend rather than a boss. But Ms Howard was also the person who wrote Mike's reference. If he wanted to get a job for next year, he had to give the impression that this one was going well.

Therefore, Mike didn't tell Judith that there were two classes which he couldn't get to stop talking, especially when they were were meant to be listening to him. Nor did he tell her that he couldn't get his year-eleven class to talk at all. Mike didn't mention how he found it almost impossible to sleep at night, and even harder to get up in the morning.

"As for discipline," Ms Howard said. "Everything OK?"

"Fine," Mike assured her. "That year-eight drama class are a bit lively, but I'm getting on top of them."

"Good, good. You know, you don't have to take them for drama every week. They're meant to have it once a fort-night. I believe Colin Scott used to give them a drama lesson when it linked in with their English work."

Now she tells me, Mike thought. They'd been pulling the wool over his eyes.

"I'm pleased that you're so keen on teaching drama," Ms Howard added. "Have you thought about what play you're going to do next term with year eleven?"

"I was thinking about *Death of a Salesman*," Mike said.

"I'm not sure we have enough copies of that in stock," the head of department said, cagily. "And I haven't budgeted to buy more. Have you considered doing Shakespeare?"

"He's the other obvious choice," Mike replied.

"We have plenty of copies of *Romeo and Juliet*."

This wasn't a play which Mike knew well, or liked.

"I think I'd prefer to do *Macbeth* or *Caesar*."

His head of department frowned. "The thing about *Romeo and Juliet*," she said, "is that I'm putting on a production of it at the end of next term, which I expect some members of year eleven will get involved with. I'll be advertising auditions next week."

"I see," Mike said.

"Therefore, it would be useful if both English top groups were studying the play – it would help the actors to understand their parts – as well, of course, as providing an audience."

"In that case," Mike said, "I'll be glad to teach ..."

Ms Howard gave him a friendly smile and stood up. "Excellent," she said, "and I would greatly appreciate any time that you could give to the play: helping people learn lines, that kind of thing. Your predecessor, Mr Scott, was always very helpful."

"Of course," Mike said, standing too. "Though commuting to Sheffield makes it difficult for me to stay after school."

"But you'll be moving to Nottingham, surely?"

"I don't know," Mike replied. "You see, I have a rela-tionship in Sheffield, and this job's only temporary ..."

His voice trailed off. Ms Howard smiled enigmatically.

"I believe the Head said the job was temporary *in the first instance.* There's no reason why you shouldn't get a permanent contract, presuming that things work out this year. Which I'm sure they will. Think about it.''

Mike drove home, quickly hitting the early Friday rush hour. In the bumper-to-bumper queue for the motorway, he had plenty of time to consider his conversation with Ms Howard. The message was clear: if he wanted a job for next year, he ought to help out with the play. But did Mike want a job at Stonywood? Hardly. Emma had another year at university after this one. Mike wanted to return to Sheffield and teach at an 11–18 school or a sixth-form college. All he needed out of Stonywood was a decent reference. So he would teach *Romeo and Juliet*, do the odd bit of line bashing at lunchtimes. But that was all. It ought to be enough.

In the flat he found a note from Emma. *Something came up. Gone home for weekend. See you Monday. X. E.* Mike groaned. Emma was mad with him because he had forgotten to phone her last night. Tired after the parents' evening, he'd gone for a drink with Phil, whose house he was staying at. They'd spent the whole evening talking about school and not left the pub until closing time. It was the first night he and Emma had spent apart in ages, but Mike hadn't thought about her when he got in. He'd fallen asleep the moment his head hit the pillow. It was the best night's sleep he'd got since starting at Stonywood.

Mike couldn't blame Emma for being annoyed. They'd been together for so long, it was easy to forget that Emma was only twenty. She wanted more from a relationship than someone who worked late every night and had little energy left for the weekend. He'd make it up to her when she got back, he promised himself, before lying down on the bed, fully dressed, and falling into a dull, dreamless sleep.

Nine

Rachel stood on the doorstep, kissing Nick goodbye. She almost invited him in, but something made her hold back. It was ten-past-eleven. Her boyfriend walked to the end of the street and gave a little wave as he turned the corner. Rachel waved back, then let herself into the house, shutting out the cold night behind her.

"I'm home."

Mum sat in the front room, reading a novel.

"You've been home for five minutes," she said. "I could hear you outside. Why didn't you invite him in? I wouldn't have minded."

Rachel shrugged. "Because I'm not ready to, I guess."

"Not because you didn't want him to meet me?"

"Course not."

Though maybe that was part of it. Having a boy turn up at Dad's was a way of rubbing his nose in it: *look, I've got my own man, I don't need you any more*. But that wasn't the message which Rachel wanted to give to Mum.

"Are you going to tell me about him?" Mum said. "It's been two Saturday nights on the trot – you *are* going out with him, aren't you?"

"I guess so," Rachel admitted.

"How long have you known him?"

"He's in my year, so, since I started going to Stonywood, I suppose. But I didn't use to like him much."

"What changed your mind?"

Rachel thought about it. Had she changed her mind? She felt more like she'd suspended judgement.

"I don't know," she told Mum. "Nick seems very young in some ways. He can be a bit of a show off. But he's actually quite shy, when you get to know him. And he's interested in acting. We have things in common."

"More than you did with Carl?"

Mum never met Carl, but Rachel had talked to her about him.

"I guess."

"You seem uncertain."

"I wish Nick was a bit older, and we didn't go to the same school."

Mum seemed confused. "Why?"

Rachel tried to explain. "Hardly any girls at school go out with boys in the same year. You know what people are like."

"I don't see the problem. If you like him enough, you'll put up with a certain amount of teasing."

"I guess."

Rachel sat down. "Is there anything good on TV?" she asked.

"One other thing," Mum said. "I know we discussed this last year but ..."

Rachel groaned. "Mum, I only kissed him for the first time tonight. I don't need a refresher course on contraception. I'll know what to do when I'm ready."

"That's what I thought," Mum said.

She left the subject there.

Rachel put the late film on, but didn't really watch it. And instead of thinking about Nick, she found herself thinking about her parents.

Mum and Dad met at a university disco when Mum was nineteen and Dad twenty-two. Mum got pregnant during her second year at university and they married in the summer. Mum dropped out of college and had Rachel. Dad stayed on and got his PhD. Mum meant to finish her degree once Rachel started school. But, that year, Dad left her for another woman. Mum couldn't afford to study. Instead, she got a job to help support herself and her daughter.

Sometimes, Rachel found it awkward, discussing relationships with Mum. They rarely talked about the divorce. Dad, when he mentioned it, said they were both too young when they married, but that couldn't be all there was to it. Clarissa was young – only twenty when Dad married her – and they'd stayed together for seven years already. Mum's boyfriends always seemed to let her down. She hadn't had one for a while. The older you were, the harder it got, for a woman. Mum said she didn't miss having a man around. But she must miss being taken out, someone making a fuss of her. Rachel's having a boyfriend was bound to rub salt into that wound.

Could Rachel fall in love with Nick? She wasn't sure. From the way he held her, from the tentative way he kissed her on the doorstep tonight, she could tell that he wasn't experienced with girls. Maybe Rachel was the first one he'd ever kissed. She wasn't sure if she liked that or not. The hard, cynical part of Rachel said he was too young for her, too naive. But her softer side said that he was real, and so obviously cared for her. She would see what happened. Sometimes you had to trust your feelings and go with them, wherever they led.

Or didn't.

Ten

The notices went up on Monday lunchtime. Rachel and Becky saw the first one on their way to registration. Reading it made Rachel late.

"*Romeo and Juliet*," Becky said. "We're starting that in English soon."

"I'd love to be in it," Rachel sighed.

"I can see the casting now," Becky mused. "You as Juliet, Nick as Romeo: a marriage made in heaven."

The second bell went before Rachel could think of a witty reply. Becky rushed to registration. Rachel couldn't be bothered. She sometimes skipped registration after spending lunchtime at Nick's. Nothing ever happened. She went straight to her first lesson of the afternoon.

She was the first to arrive. Mr Steadman was in the room when Rachel walked in. He smiled at her. It felt odd, being in the room alone with him. To fill the hollow air, she asked him about the play.

"Are those notices up already?" he asked her. "Ms Howard asked me to tell you about the production. I was going to do it today."

"Could I borrow a copy, sir?" she asked, making a sudden decision. "I'd like to read it before the auditions next week."

"No need," he told her. "We'll be starting the play today. I've just got the stock-cupboard keys from Ms Howard so that I can collect the books. Would you give me a hand carrying them up here?"

Rachel followed the teacher to the stock cupboard on the floor below.

"Have you ever done any acting?" Steadman asked on the way.

"I was in the school production last year," she told him. "*Bugsy Malone.*"

"And who did you play?"

"A gangster's moll."

He gave her a surprised look. "I can't picture you as a floozie, somehow."

Rachel smiled. "You'd be surprised what a bit of make-up and a wig can do."

"I'm sure."

The stock cupboard was behind an insignificant door near the drama studio. Inside, though, it was huge. Rachel followed the teacher into the room.

"Any idea where I'd find *Romeo and Juliet*?" Mr Steadman asked Rachel. "I've not been in here before."

"I wouldn't know where to begin."

"Me neither. But a lightswitch would help."

Rachel fumbled around near the door. "Here."

The light came on.

"That's better," Mr Steadman said.

The space between the bookshelves was cramped. They were standing very close together. The teacher looked uncomfortable.

"Perhaps you wouldn't mind waiting outside the door, Rachel," he said, with a boyish grin. "We don't want people to talk."

"Sure," Rachel smiled back, feeling like she'd been paid a compliment.

From inside the stockroom, the teacher gave a running commentary on the books he was rummaging through.

"Oxford Secondary English. *The Outsiders. I Am The Cheese* – what on earth's that? *Creatures Moving*. There's some weird things in here. *The Art of English* – that ought to have gone in the flood. *The Long, the Short and the Tall* – at least we're getting to plays now. Ah ha, *Macbeth, A Midsummer Night's Dream* and yes, here it is, *Romeo and Juliet*."

He counted out fifteen copies and gave them to Rachel, then counted out a similar number to carry back himself.

"And what part did you have in mind?" Mr Steadman asked, as he closed the door behind him, then locked it.

"I don't know," Rachel said. "Something small, I guess."

"Why?" the teacher asked. "I marked your first essay last night. It was really good. Perceptive. If you act half as well as you write ..."

Rachel flushed with pride.

"Thanks," she said.

Back in the classroom, Steadman gave back the essays. He'd given Rachel an A. She'd never had an A before. Mr Scott was always stingy with them. The best he'd ever given Rachel was a B+, which was what Becky got today. As Mr Steadman was handing out copies of the play, everybody compared marks. No one else had done as well as Rachel, not even Nick.

Steadman started talking about *Romeo and Juliet*. It was written at about the same time as *A Midsummer Night's Dream*, he said, and covered several of the same themes, but in a more serious way.

"For instance, there's this boy, Romeo, and, at the beginning, he's crazy about a girl called Rosaline. However, by the end of the first act, he's fallen for Juliet and Rosaline isn't mentioned again. This could be the material for a comedy, like *Dream*, about how fickle young lovers' hearts are. But this isn't a comedy, it's a tragedy. Juliet is forbidden fruit. Anyone know why?"

"Is it because she's under age, sir?" Lisa Sharpe suggested.

A couple of people laughed.

"Actually," Steadman said, "today, she would be. Juliet's not quite fourteen at the beginning of the play. Romeo's age isn't made clear. He's probably older, but still in his teens."

"When were you allowed to get married at that time?" Becky asked.

"Girls as young as thirteen married then, but fourteen would still have been seen as unusual. Sixteen or seventeen would be the norm. However, Juliet's the most eligible girl in Verona, so there's pressure on her parents to marry her off as early as possible."

"And how old would the bloke she marries be?" Lisa asked.

"Convention would make him much older than Romeo. Late twenties mostly. Older, some of the time."

Lisa made a face.

"Anyway," Steadman went on, "the reason that Romeo and Juliet's love was forbidden is that they belong to rival families. He's a Montague. She's a Capulet. *Two households, both alike in dignity*, but bitter enemies."

Rachel wasn't listening. She already knew the story of *Romeo and Juliet*. Mum had made her watch the animated version when she was still at primary school. But Rachel wasn't thinking about the play itself. She was thinking about what the teacher said earlier. Could she play Juliet?

All the school's most experienced actors, the ones who competed for the main parts in previous productions, had now left. Rachel couldn't think of anyone better qualified than her in year eleven. There might be some talented people in year ten, of course. In fact, Mr Steadman had just said that Juliet was only fourteen, so even girls in year nine might be in with a chance. But Rachel could make herself look younger as well as older.

Acting in the play might interfere with her exams. But the notice said that the production was on at the end of the Spring term. She would have Easter to revise in and, anyway, doing the play would help with the English Literature exam. She wondered if Nick was interested in . . .

Her thoughts were interrupted by a knock on the door. Rachel looked up to see Mrs Bethell, her form tutor, walking into the room.

"Excuse me, Mr Steadman, have you got Rachel Webster in here?"

"Yes."

"Could I have a word with her outside, please?"

Reluctantly, Rachel left the room. Mrs Bethell wore a serious expression. Rachel worried. Suppose Mum had been taken ill? But there was no sympathy in Mrs Bethell's voice when she spoke to her.

"Do you know what this is about, Rachel?"

"No, Miss."

"You're in trouble."

Mrs Bethell took the register out of her bag and opened it to the third week in November.

"Three days in a row you've missed afternoon registration. You know, Rachel, usually truants in year eleven do the opposite of what you're doing. They turn up to register, then skive off the rest of the afternoon."

Rachel apologized. "I didn't think it made any difference. I'm always on time for my lessons."

"It makes a big difference," Mrs Bethell explained, sternly. "You're affecting the school's unofficial absences statistics. And you're making me miss part of my free period. So I'm afraid, young lady, you're in trouble."

"What kind of trouble?"

"Since this is your first offence, I'm going to count this as three lates, rather than truanting. That's an automatic Head's detention. Tomorrow's is already full, so yours will have to be a week on Thursday."

Rachel shrugged acceptance as Mrs Bethell walked away. She'd never had a Head's detention before. It felt silly to be getting one now, in her final year. But it wouldn't hurt. All it meant was an extra forty minutes after school on ...

"Hold on!" she called out to her form tutor.

"What is it, Rachel?"

"I can't go next Thursday, Miss. It's the auditions for the play. Can't you make it the week after?"

Mrs Bethell shook her head.

"I've already put the form in, Rachel. You should have thought of that when you decided to skip afternoon registration."

Rachel went back into the classroom, where Mr Steadman was getting the group to chant the prologue to *Romeo and Juliet*. They were repeating the lines again and again, until they got the metre right. Rachel, seething with frustration, listened silently, oblivious to the words and what they meant. Mr Steadman gave her a reproachful glance, disappointed that she wasn't joining in.

Eleven

Rachel was surprised when, on Tuesday, instead of reading the play, Mr Steadman brought in a video. Normally, when teachers showed videos, it was as an end of term treat. But there were four weeks to go. In the film, a gay man used the Auden poem that the class were studying as a eulogy for his dead lover.

Mr Steadman gave a definition of a eulogy.

"What about a definition of *love*, sir?" Nick asked. "Do all writers mean the same thing when they use the word?"

"Love's a pretty subjective thing," Steadman said. "That is, it means different things to different people."

Next to Rachel, Becky gave a cynical frown.

"What about you, sir?" Kate Duerden piped up. "Have you ever been in love?"

Steadman winced. You didn't ask teachers that kind of question.

"Let me try to clarify," he said, with the put-on voice he used when he was getting too intellectual for the class. "We usually draw a distinction," he went on, "between *loving* somebody, and being *in love*. When we talk about love, we're often talking about the latter state, which most people agree is transitory, something which happens at the beginning of a relationship."

Rachel smiled, enjoying the way the teacher had ducked

Kate's question about his love life. Nick, though, was like a dog with a bone.

"I don't see the difference, sir," he said. "Why can't they be one and the same thing? Like, in the poem, the guy's saying that he was wrong to think that love lasts for ever, but he isn't wrong because love can't last a lifetime. He's wrong because his lover died."

Rachel squirmed, worrying that part of Nick's performance was for her benefit. People might realize. So far, only Becky and Carmen knew that she was going out with Nick.

"Maybe you're right, Nick," Steadman replied. "Maybe we need to agree on a definition of love before we go any further. The transitory thing I was talking about – the first flush of love – might be better described as a crush, or sexual obsession. There's also a deeper, almost religious sense in which we use the word and – yes – we'd all like to think that it can last for ever, although divorce statistics tell a somewhat different tale."

The bell went, and the teacher looked relieved.

"You'd better watch Nick," Becky told Rachel, as they left school. "You heard what he said: when he mates, he mates for life."

Rachel laughed uncomfortably.

"Hey, look, sir's got a new car," a voice called out as Mike was finishing for the day on Tuesday afternoon. It was Paul Wilks, the cheekiest member of Mike's year-seven group. Paul could talk up a storm, but had trouble writing a sentence.

"Well, not so new, actually," Paul added. "I preferred the old one, sir. What happened to it?"

"I didn't own that one, Paul. This is mine."

Mike looked ruefully at the ten-year-old Ford Escort, its various bumps and scratches touched up with paint which didn't quite match. Then he got in and drove back to Sheffield, thinking all the while about the past few days.

On Saturday, he'd bought the Escort from an ad in the Nottingham Evening Post. With Emma away, there'd been no one he wanted to see in Sheffield. His friends from the PGCE course had all moved away and Emma's friends were ... Emma's friends. So he'd arranged to visit Phil on Saturday and stay over. Phil had helped him to choose the car, then driven Mike's Escort over to Sheffield on Sunday while Mike returned Emma's Peugeot.

"Nice place," Phil commented, as he looked round the flat. "Is that Emma?" He was pointing at a photograph over the fireplace. Mike nodded modestly.

"She's lovely. You're a lucky guy."

They drove back to Nottingham together and Mike stayed another night there. Phil's house was rapidly becoming his second home. He wished that he'd stayed there on Monday night, too, because, when he got in on Monday evening, there'd been a message from Emma on the machine, saying that she wouldn't be back till Tuesday. He tried to ring and find out why, but his girlfriend wasn't in.

At least he'd got a lot of work done last night. Without Emma there, wanting attention, concentration was easier. And he'd slept well. Today, every single one of Mike's lessons had gone OK. Usually, there was at least one disaster. Even the last lesson of the afternoon was pretty good. Mike's year-eleven group enjoyed the extract from *Four Weddings and a Funeral*. For once, they'd got a decent class discussion going. Mike felt that he was beginning to build a rapport with them.

Driving home took longer in the Escort. It seemed even longer because the car had no radio or cassette player. Mike worried that the car wasn't up to making the trip ten times a week. At least Emma would be pleased that he no longer needed to borrow hers.

She was there when he got in, sitting at the kitchen table, working on an essay. He was about to tell her how much he'd missed her, but Emma got in first.

"How come you didn't take my car to work today? Something wrong with it?"

Mike explained. Instead of being pleased, his girlfriend seemed annoyed.

"Why didn't you come over at the weekend? I thought you might show up on Sunday at least, have dinner with Mum and Dad, drive me home."

She was being unfair. Mike protested. "Your note said *See you Monday*! I had loads of work to do on Sunday."

Emma wasn't satisfied. "You had time to go to Nottingham – which is more than halfway – and buy a car, but you didn't even have time to ring me once!"

He should have rung, Mike realized. But he'd had the feeling that Emma was annoyed with him, and he'd wanted to avoid a fight. Now he was getting the fight anyway.

"I meant to ..."

"Yeah, but you were too busy getting drunk with your teaching buddy. Maybe you ought to move in with him. You two seem to have more in common than we do these days."

Mike tried to put his arms around her. "Don't do this, Emma. This is just ..."

She burst into tears, stopping his words. Mike held her, but the tears didn't cease, smearing her make-up, giving her face a child-like vulnerability. Mike was tired. The last thing he needed was a big scene. Emma wasn't usually like this.

After a while, she stopped. Her voice became sombre. "We have to talk," she said.

Mike sat down. "What is it?"

Emma didn't look at him, which was a bad sign. When she began, her voice went up in pitch, making her sound younger. "I can't take much more of this, Mike. I'm a student. I hardly have any responsibilities. This is meant to be the best time of my life! But we never have fun any more. It's been like this all year. I feel like I'm missing out."

Mike was quiet. He understood how Emma felt. Her first term here had been great. They'd found this flat. Emma was excited to be living away from home. She liked her course and he liked his. But the following term, he'd started on teaching practice, and they'd seen a lot less of each other. Things were better in the summer. They went to the Glastonbury festival and had a couple of weeks travelling around France. But his failure to get a job had cast a pall over things. And since he'd started at Stonywood ...

"I've spent a lot of time thinking this weekend," Emma said. "And I've talked it over with Mum and Dad, and with Steve ..."

"What is it?" Mike asked.

"You know Carol?"

She was a friend of Emma's, the one she'd gone to the Sugar concert with.

"What about her?"

"There's a spare room in her house. I'm going to move into it."

"*What?*"

Mike was staggered. He'd had no idea that this was

coming. The ground shifted beneath him and, for a moment, he felt like the earth would swallow him up.

"You can't do that, Emma. I love you. We're ..."

"I'm sorry," Emma said, her face hardening. "But this isn't working. I feel like you're holding me back. You've changed this year, and I don't like it."

"People change all the time," Mike argued. "It's just that I have to live in the real world now. I have a job ..."

Emma shook her head so that the hair fell in front of her face. He couldn't see her eyes.

"I know you do," she said. "But I don't have to live in the real world yet, Mike. I feel like you're boxing me in. When I'm with you, I'm still the same person who idolized you at fifteen. I need the space to be myself."

"You can't leave," Mike said. "Not now. I'll give you space, all you need. But don't leave. I need you."

Suddenly, Emma's voice became less sympathetic. "Oh, come on, Mike. If you need me so much, why didn't you call me all weekend? And it's stupid, you living in Sheffield. This place costs a fortune. Why don't you give it up and move in with your friend, Phil?"

Mike found himself waking up. "What's going on here? Are we splitting up?"

Emma gave him a long, hard look. "Yes," she said. "I think we are."

Twelve

Rachel spent Thursday lunchtime at Nick's house, as usual. It was their first time alone together since the previous week. Rachel hadn't seen her boyfriend at the weekend, because she'd gone with Dad and his new family to visit her grandparents. It was a rotten journey. All five of them were crammed into Dad's posey Shogun. But she hadn't seen Grandad and Grandma since last Christmas and Grandad wasn't well. She felt duty bound to go.

Anyway, it wasn't her grandparents who Rachel didn't get on with, but her father and his second wife. Clarissa was in a foul mood all weekend, for no apparent reason. Phoebe and Rowan, picking this up, seemed sulky, too. Dad, by contrast, was unnaturally cheerful. He kept asking questions about Rachel and Nick until Clarissa stopped him.

"Stop it, Eric. Can't you see she doesn't want to tell you? Teenage girls don't want to discuss their love life with men your age."

Now, Rachel and Nick lay on his narrow single bed, bodies entwined. For the first time, Rachel had let Nick take off her bra. It was a wonderful feeling, his chest pressing against hers. She kissed him harder. They were both breathing deeply now, getting excited. Rachel wondered what it would be like to go further. But it was time to go back to school for afternoon registration.

Entering the building, they passed a notice for the play

auditions after school. Rachel asked Nick if he'd made up his mind whether to go for a part.

"I dunno," he said. "It's awfully close to the exams."

Rachel was in the same tutor group as Kate Duerden, who walked in a few seconds after her. Kate gave Rachel a funny look, but Rachel didn't take any notice of it. Mrs Bethell smiled when Rachel answered her name on the register. She'd now been on time for four days in a row.

In English, they read a rather long, boring scene which was mainly between Mercutio and Romeo. The teacher looked worn out, depressed.

"All right," said Mr Steadman, when it was over. "Now we get to a really crucial scene: the ball. Juliet's meant to be meeting Paris, who wants to be her husband. Instead, she encounters Romeo, who ought to be her sworn enemy. Rachel, will you read Juliet?"

Rachel nodded, happy to have the main part.

"And we'll have someone new to read Romeo. Let me see ..."

"I think you should choose Nick," Kate Duerden called out. "After all, he and Rachel spent all lunch hour practising the bedroom scene!"

Rachel blushed. Becky turned round and gave Kate a look of such ferocity that she shut up. Nick half rose out of his seat and swore at Kate.

"What business is it of yours, you stupid, silly ..."

"Ooh," Lisa Sharpe called out. "Lucky guess, Kate."

"That's enough!" Mr Steadman said.

Surprisingly, everyone shut up. Nick sat down, his face redder than Rachel's. She had never been so embarrassed in her life. How did Kate Duerden know that she and Nick had been together? A wild shot, probably, but the whole class now knew that it was a bull's-eye.

"Paul, read Romeo. Rachel, would you like someone else to take Juliet?"

"Yes, please."

Now that chance had gone. If she'd read well this afternoon, Mr Steadman might have stood up for her when she was late for the auditions tomorrow.

Nick tried to talk to Rachel after the lesson, but Rachel rushed away. She couldn't believe that, an hour before, she'd been considering losing her virginity to Nick. How could he embarrass her that way?

Thirteen

After school on Wednesday, Mike told Phil that he'd split up with Emma. He'd persuaded her to stay in the flat the night before, and tried everything he could think of to get her to change her mind. It did no good. There was only one bed, and they shared, but she wouldn't make love with him. They cuddled. They cried. Eventually, they ran out of things to say. Mike lay in bed, unable to sleep, trying to work out how it had come to this.

Phil offered him the spare room in his house. That night, while Emma moved out, Mike stayed at Phil's and slept for twelve hours solid. They agreed to move the rest of his stuff to Nottingham at the weekend. There was no point in giving notice on the flat. With Mike being paid in arrears, he and Emma were already behind with the rent. He'd post the keys through the letting agent's door.

By Thursday afternoon, Mike didn't know whether he was coming or going. He'd forgotten the auditions for the play, which he'd rashly agreed to attend. But Judith Howard strode over to see him at afternoon break.

"Once we've got them settled down, I'd like you to look at the older ones, Mike. Get them to read a short passage from the play. Then, if there's time, I'll have them all act a short piece in pairs."

"Are you going to cast the main parts today?" Mike asked.

"Lord, no. We'll come up with a shortlist, that's all. Though I've got a few ideas. Has anyone from your year-eleven group said they're coming?"

"I tried to persuade Rachel Webster. She's very talented."

Judith seemed to recognize the name. "Oh, yes, the governor's daughter."

"Pardon?"

"Her mother's one of the school governors, but I've never taught the girl. What about Nick Cowan?"

"Can he act?"

Judith Howard gave Mike a condescending you-don't-really-know-your-students smile. "He was in the Edinburgh Festival earlier this year. But he's never been involved in a school production. I don't know why. We could certainly use him."

Mike thought about Nick Cowan as he walked over to the hall for the auditions. He'd been surprised, this afternoon, at Nick's reaction to Kate Duerden's teasing. The only conclusion to draw was that what Kate said was true, or – judging by Rachel Webster's red face – at least partly true. Mike felt odd about it. Rachel was fast becoming his favourite in the class. In his upset state, Mike could almost admit to himself that he fancied the girl. But only in an abstract way. He thought of Rachel as attractive, intelligent and innocent. Even – yes – virginal. It seemed wrong that she should already be having sex. Yet, statistically, many girls her age did, Mike knew that. What did Rachel see in Nick Cowan? Maybe the boy really did have hidden depths.

When he got to the auditions, Rachel wasn't there. Mike was disappointed. He helped Judith to organize the fifty or so students waiting in the vast, cold assembly hall. Judith gave a speech about self-discipline, asking the younger kids to keep quiet during each audition. But there was never a chance that she would succeed. There were too many exuberant eleven and twelve year olds. Few of them had the slightest chance of getting one of the twenty-two parts.

Nick Cowan turned up ten minutes late, looking around nervously. Mike called him over to join the twenty other upper school hopefuls. But before he got to them, Judith Howard came over. Joyce Jones had arrived and taken control of the younger kids.

"No need for you to stay," Judith told Nick. "The auditions for the main parts are on Tuesday lunchtime. Decide two that you want to go for and learn a speech for each."

"All right," Nick said. He was looking around to see if Rachel was there, Mike realized. This was probably his main reason for turning up. Nick didn't need the play. It needed him. He would only be in it if Rachel was, too. And who could blame him?

Mike and Judith Howard listened to twenty students read a dozen or so lines. At the end of it, Ms Howard dismissed nearly half of them, including Lisa Sharpe from his year-eleven group.

"Sorry," Judith told them, without any real sympathy in her voice. "You haven't got it yet. Please leave quietly."

Then the remaining twelve began reading bits of the play in pairs. Some were much better than others. None were great. For Mike, in his tired state, they began to blur into each other. It was gone half-four when Rachel Webster rushed into the room. Mike woke up.

"Sorry I'm late," she blurted out. "I had a ..."

"If you can't be on time," Ms Howard said, curtly, "then you've no chance of being involved."

Rachel's face fell. Mike went over to her as she turned away.

"Hold on," he said, gently putting a hand on her shoulder. "Why are you late?"

Rachel told him. Mike went over and spoke to Judith. "She had a detention for some trivial thing. Her form tutor knew about the audition but refused to let her out of it. I think we ought to give her a chance. She's the girl I told you about before. The governor's daughter."

Judith wouldn't want to upset one of the school governors by not allowing her daughter to audition.

"Very well," Judith said, "but she'll need a partner to audition with."

"I can partner her," Mike offered.

He went over to Rachel and told her what they'd agreed.

"Thank you, sir," Rachel said. "You're brilliant."

He saw her looking around, probably checking if Nick was there. She didn't seem disappointed when he wasn't.

"Choose a passage with two people speaking," Mike told her. "Not the balcony scene. People keep doing that. I'll come over and practise with you in five minutes."

When he came back, Rachel had chosen the second half of the scene where, warned by the nurse, Romeo flees from Juliet's bedroom.

"All right," said Mike. "You know what's happened here? Have you read the play?"

"I know the story," Rachel said. "They've made love for the first time. It's morning, and Romeo's overslept."

Mike liked the way Rachel said "made love" rather than something cruder.

"Fine," he said. "Let's take it from line forty-one."

Rachel read, *"Then, window, let day in, and let life out."*

It was a good choice of scene. Juliet had more lines than Romeo but she also had plenty of opportunities to react. Rachel read competently. When they'd finished, Mike told her to emote a little more.

"Let's do it another time."

"Mr Steadman," Judith Howard's voice interrupted. "We're ready for you."

"Give it your best shot," Mike whispered to Rachel.

In front of the other students, Mike felt like he was auditioning, too. He read his part with unvarnished sincerity, omitting the kiss referred to in the first line. Rachel read with nervous passion. Then Ms Howard read a bit of Lady Capulet's part, making Rachel continue beyond the point she'd rehearsed. She stumbled a little, but didn't do badly, considering.

"Thank you," Judith said, when Rachel got to the bit where Juliet denounces Romeo as a villain for killing her cousin. She turned to the whole room. "That concludes the auditions. Most of you will get parts of some kind. I'll put a notice up tomorrow, saying which people we'd like to come back on Tuesday lunchtime to read for the main roles."

When the kids were all gone, Mike sat down with Joyce and Judith to discuss the casting. They decided which boys were the main contenders for the main parts.

"I'm hoping that Nick Cowan will read for Romeo," Judith said. "If he won't take on such a big role, he'd make an excellent Tybalt."

They discussed other contenders for Romeo, but none seemed as strong. Then the discussion moved on to the girls. Joyce suggested a year-nine girl, Marie Foulks, for Juliet.

"That is very young," Judith said.

"She's the same age as Juliet is in the play," Joyce argued.

"I know. But there're an awful lot of lines for her to learn."

"Nowhere near as many as Romeo."

"We'll audition her with the older ones, but don't build her hopes up. Mike, what did you think of Michelle Harper?"

Mike hesitated, trying to be objective. "She read confidently. I can't quite see her as Juliet, though. She's a bit ... I don't know what the politically correct term is."

"You can say what you like," Judith said. "Tarty?"

"Something like that," Mike agreed.

"You're right. I think she might make a good Rosaline, but not Juliet. How about Sarah Smythe?"

"I don't remember her."

"Long hair, skinny, strong voice: performed the scene with the nurse."

"So-so."

Judith nodded. "Worth a second glance, maybe. I thought that her partner, Maxine, made a good nurse. But Juliet's going to be difficult. Maybe we should take a closer look at this year-nine girl."

Mike hesitated before speaking. "What about Rachel Webster?"

"I was coming to her," Judith said. "She's quite a mature-looking girl, isn't she? She read reasonably. I was thinking of her as Lady Capulet."

"You weren't convinced by her as Juliet?"

Judith gave him a hard look. *I shouldn't be seen to be playing favourites*, Mike thought.

"I'm not convinced by any of them as Juliet," Ms Howard said. "It's whether I see the potential for them to *become* Juliet. Rachel read reasonably. Her face might fit. But we could have a problem with her looking older than our potential Romeos.''

"Surely that's down to the make-up," Mike commented. "It's just that ..." He made a snap decision to tell Judith something that might sway her. "She's Nick Cowan's girl-friend. So you may get some interesting sexual chemistry there."

Judith raised a curious eyebrow. "Romance on the set often creates more problems than it resolves, Mike. But that's useful to know. Rachel's presence in a big role might entice Nick to take one himself."

After five minutes, it was agreed that Nick and Rachel were to go on to the list for the following Tuesday, along with seven others. Mike hoped that he'd done the young lovers a favour.

"Why do you want to be in the play so much?" Becky asked Rachel on Friday lunchtime. "Is it because of Nick?"

"Nick wasn't even at the auditions."

Rachel didn't tell Becky how confused her feelings about Nick were. They were on their way over to the drama studio, where the list for Tuesday's audition was meant to be up. Rachel had already checked the noticeboard at the begin-ning of lunchtime, but the notice hadn't been there.

"Are you holding out on me?" Becky asked. "Is there something else?"

"I want to be an actress," Rachel told Becky. "I want the experience."

One of the frustrating things about going to a small school like Stonywood was that it didn't offer drama at GCSE. Rachel intended to do the A-level at college. She'd men-tioned it to Mr Steadman and he'd said it was a good idea.

In the corridor outside the studio, Ms Howard was pinning a notice on the board.

"Ah, Rachel," she said, "I'm glad I saw you."

She's going to say she's sorry, but I wasn't good enough, Rachel thought. She found the head of English frosty and intimidating.

"You'll see you're on this list," Ms Howard said.

"That's ... great." Surprised, Rachel tried not to sound too excited.

"You'll also see that I ask each person on it to prepare two parts. I'd like you to read for Juliet and her mother, Lady Capulet. Is that understood?"

"Yes."

"I'll see you on Tuesday. If the audition overruns, you'll be allowed to miss the first lesson of the afternoon. I'll make that clear to Mrs Bethell." So Ms Howard knew why Rachel was late for last night's audition. That was good. Rachel read the other names on the list. The only one which meant much to her was Nick's. How come he was on there when he hadn't been at the audition?

"Lady Capulet," Becky repeated as they left the building. "You'd enjoy that, wouldn't you – standing around while some other girl necks with Nick."

"It's only acting," Rachel said. Becky gave a knowing look in return.

As they walked to registration, Rachel saw Nick.

"Have you seen the audition notice?" she asked him.

He shook his head.

"You're on it."

"Miss Howard said I would be." He didn't seem surprised, or flattered.

"Do you know what you're going to read for yet?"

"Haven't thought about it. Why don't we discuss it tomorrow?"

Rachel didn't reply immediately. She and Nick hadn't seen each other alone since the embarrassing incident the previous afternoon. Afterwards, Rachel had almost decided to chuck Nick. Kate's comment wasn't his fault, but he'd reacted like a child, showing both of them up. Yet part of Rachel still wanted Nick. She wanted what Becky dropped hints about: the thrill of sex. And love, if such a thing existed. Rachel wanted to know what being in love felt like. She guessed she'd know it when she found it.

Or would she? Nick was standing in front of her now and Rachel felt no lust, never mind love. She felt uncomfortable and a little afraid.

"You *are* free this weekend?" he asked, less confidently.

"I think so," she said. "Give me a ring in the morning."

"You played that rather cool," Becky said, as Nick left. "Going off him?"

Rachel didn't reply. Becky could read what she wanted into her silence.

Fourteen

Nick wanted Rachel to go round to his house at the weekend, but she refused. She hadn't met his parents before, and didn't want to now. She told him she had to do some Christmas shopping, even though it was only early December. They could meet in town that afternoon. When Nick suggested other times, Rachel told him she was busy in the evening and had schoolwork all day Sunday.

"I thought I worked hard, until I got to know you," Nick said, on the phone. But Rachel wasn't telling the truth about the hours she worked. Nick was. That was another thing which made her uncomfortable with him. Nick was too conscientious about school. He took everything so seriously.

They met at Barrio, a big, airy tapas bar above the Hippo Club where Rachel went sometimes, although she was under age. Nick tried to talk about the play, but it was the last thing that Rachel wanted to discuss.

"Ms Howard wants me to play Romeo," he said, as though it was an imposition, rather than an honour. "But it's too big a role. If I was doing it, I'd miss a load of lessons and never get up to speed on revision before Easter. So I think I'll go for Tybalt instead. He's got a nice juicy part, but then he gets killed, so I wouldn't be in the majority of rehearsals. How about you? What are you going for?"

Rachel expected Nick to assume she would go for Juliet. But he didn't. He acted like the lead role would be his for the taking but she would have to audition for a menial one.

"Ms Howard wants me to audition for Lady Capulet," she told Nick. Half-listening, he asked for a refill of coffee. He didn't need more caffeine, Rachel thought. He was hyper enough already.

"That'd be good," Nick said. "Lady C's mainly in the early parts of the play, too. We'd be at some of the same rehearsals."

Rachel paused. "She's also asked me to audition for Juliet."

"Really?" Nick thanked the waiter. "That's a big role."

"Nowhere near as big as Romeo."

"I don't know," Nick said, with a sly smile. "If you're going for Juliet, maybe I should go for Romeo."

"I don't think so," Rachel said, absentmindedly sipping the dregs of her cappuccino. "After all, as you say, it's a huge part. Also, Romeo and Juliet aren't in it together that much – I think there are only four scenes or so."

Nick smiled and stroked her hand. "But I can't have some other guy kissing you," he said.

Rachel removed her hand from his. She looked around the spacious bar to see how private they were. The lunch-time rush was over. There were three other couples at tables. The handsome barman was chatting up an attractive woman who was too young for him. Rachel turned back to Nick. He looked painfully earnest.

"What's wrong?" he asked.

"I think you should take whatever part you want," Rachel said. "I'll take whatever I can get."

"Have I offended you somehow?"

"No, it's not that . . ."

Nick shook his head. He had a penetrating gaze when he wanted. Its intensity unsettled her. "You thought I was being jealous?" he asked.

Rachel tried to explain. "You're the experienced actor. You know what happens on stage isn't real."

Nick began to speak quickly, his words tumbling over one another. "All I meant was – if you get to play Juliet, then I'd rather be the guy playing Romeo. Everything else may be acting, but the kisses are real. I know, 'a kiss is just a kiss,' but I want to be the only one kissing you."

Rachel shook her head. Part of her wanted to manufacture a row with Nick, to give her an excuse to walk out. But that would be too cruel. "If that's really the way you feel, tell him the truth," Mum had counselled when they discussed it last night. Mum had told Rachel that she was being immature – pulling out at the first sign of trouble. But Rachel had made up her mind.

"What is it?" Nick asked, putting his hand over hers. "What's wrong?"

"This doesn't feel right," Rachel said.

"What do you mean?"

"Us." She took her hand away.

"But, on Thursday, we ..."

"I don't want to talk about Thursday."

"I don't understand."

Rachel hated herself. She wasn't this cruel, heartless person. It was only a character she was playing. But she didn't know any other way to behave. How did you finish with someone? She'd never done it before.

"This isn't working," Rachel told him, fumbling in her purse, no longer sure what she was saying. "I should never have gone out with you in the first place."

"Why not?" Nick pleaded. "What have I done? What do you want?"

"I don't know," Rachel said, conscious that a couple of people were turning round to look at them. "I don't know what I want. All I know is, you're not it. I'm sorry, Nick."

Rachel slammed a pound coin down on the table to pay for her coffee. Eyes watering, she hurried out of the bar.

Nick still had to pay for the coffees. She had a minute's grace. Rachel ran across Middle Pavement, into the entrance of the Broadmarsh Shopping Centre. She took the escalator down, then hurried past the Caves of Nottingham exhibit and Forbidden Planet comic shop. The second escalator took her into the mob of Saturday afternoon shoppers. Rachel let them carry her along until she stopped outside C&A, making the Christmas crowd part around her. The shoppers were all too preoccupied to notice the fifteen-year-old girl in the middle of them, wiping the smudged make-up from her sad face.

Fifteen

"Where's Nick Cowan?" Judith Howard asked on Tuesday lunchtime, five minutes after the final auditions were due to begin.

"He was off school yesterday," Mike told her. "Still ill, I presume."

"That puts a spanner in the works," Judith complained. "But I suppose we'd better get on with it."

There were eight people auditioning, four of each sex. Michelle Harper was quickly cast as Rosaline. She'd wanted to be Juliet, but seemed happy. That left Marie Foulks from year nine and two girls from year eleven: Rachel Webster and Sarah Smythe. The three were equally matched. Rachel was the best-looking in Mike's eyes, but Sarah Smythe had the better voice. Marie had a grating voice, Mike thought, but was very confident and manifestly younger than the other girls, which would give the production an interesting angle. Marie was also more experienced. Nick could see that Judith was tilting towards casting her. He and Joyce Jones had a say in the casting, but Joyce also liked the younger girl.

The four boys were all reasonable. None stood out. Stuart Bentley might make a good Tybalt. Paul Johnson would do as Mercutio. A rather overweight boy called Troy Martin seemed to cast himself as Friar Lawrence. A potentially handsome but rather bland-looking boy called Mark

Kepper clearly thought he had the part of Romeo in the bag. Mike thought he would be better cast as Paris, the older man who Juliet's parents want her to marry. They were still short of a Romeo, a Benvolio, Capulet and Montague. The two fathers weren't crucial parts, but even if Nick Cowan agreed to play Romeo, they were one down.

"Perhaps we could have Mike play Paris?" Joyce suggested. "He's the right sort of age."

"It's a thought," Judith said. "I've cast staff in productions before."

"I'm not an actor," Mike protested.

"You seemed very confident with Rachel the other day," Judith told him, but Mike was relieved when she didn't press the idea.

They continued trying the auditioners in new combinations. It was clear that Rachel or Sarah would make a good Lady Capulet, but doubts were beginning to creep in about Marie Foulks. She was one of those arrogant kids who did a drama workshop every weekend and thought she knew better than the teachers what "real" acting was.

"I think she might get on my nerves," Judith Howard confessed in one of their frequent conferences. "Let's try Rachel again. Joyce, could you have a go at her face – do something with her hair, too?"

Joyce Jones went and made Rachel up. Marie Foulks, seeing this, looked like she was about to go nuclear. When Rachel returned, her hair brushed back, face paler and lips painted a narrow, pale pink, she looked younger than Marie, and much more innocent. Judith got Rachel to change her voice slightly, so that it was more like that of a precocious child than a woman. Mike thought that she was perfect.

"I'm still not sure," Judith said. "Rachel looks the part,

but I don't know if she's an experienced enough actress. She's only had bit parts before."

"I think she's good enough," Mike said, though he had nothing but his own intuition to base it on.

"I don't know Rachel well enough," Joyce commented, tactfully, "but I'm sure that Marie would shape up. We could knock the attitude out of her."

Judith called the three girls to her.

"Sarah, we'd like you to play Lady Capulet."

"Thanks, Miss."

The other two girls looked like the nervous finalists in a beauty contest. Rachel glanced at Mike for reassurance. He smiled sympathetically back, but couldn't offer her any. He didn't know what Judith had decided.

"We all liked both of you two girls," Ms Howard said, "and it's a very difficult choice. We'd like one of you to play Juliet and the other to act as understudy. But I'm afraid we can't decide which one of you until we've cast Romeo. I promise we'll have a decision by the end of the week."

Marie and Rachel groaned. The two girls didn't look at each other. Mike guessed that it was demeaning for Rachel, being in competition with a girl two years younger. They left, and Judith went over for a final word with the boys. It was nearly afternoon break. Mike, Judith and Joyce were free because they usually had an English department meeting at this time, but they all had to teach after break. The boys left, parts not yet finalized. The teachers were about to go, too, when Nick Cowan poked his head through the door.

"Where have *you* been?" Judith Howard asked, not trying to hide her annoyance.

"Off sick, Miss. I was feeling a bit better this afternoon,

so I came in. I wanted to apologize for missing the audition."

"It's only just finished," Judith said. "You could have come along."

"Sorry," Nick said, sheepishly. "I thought it was on at lunchtime."

"Sit down," Judith said. "We might still have a part for you."

Nick looked reluctant. He was far too polite to risk offending his teachers, Mike decided, but he wasn't all that bothered about being in the play, either.

"What role did you have in mind?" Judith asked him.

"I didn't want anything too big," Nick said, "not with exams coming up. I thought, maybe, Tybalt."

"We've already cast Tybalt," Ms Howard said, though this wasn't strictly true.

"Oh. What's left then?"

Judith glanced at Mike for support. She wanted him to hook Nick, then reel him in. Mike found himself playing along.

"There's Romeo's father, Montague, and Juliet's father, Capulet," Mike said, matter of factly. "Neither of those is a big role. The other part which we haven't made a definite decision on is Romeo himself."

Nick's eyes met Mike's. The boy had an intense gaze which Mike found a little unnerving.

"Who's Juliet?" he asked.

"That can't be decided until we know who's playing Romeo. It's between Rachel and another girl, Marie Foulks."

"I know Marie," Nick said. "She was in Edinburgh with us this year."

"Are you interested?" Mike asked.

"I would be, if it wasn't for the exams," Nick said.

"The play will be over the week before Easter," Judith Howard assured him. "You'd have plenty of time for revision, I promise."

"If I took the part," Nick asked, "would I have a say in who got to play Juliet?"

The cheek of it, Mike thought. Nick was almost blackmailing them. He would only play Romeo if his girlfriend got to play Juliet.

"We'd welcome your opinion, Nick," Ms Howard said. "But mine is the final decision. And, if my decision happens to be the same as yours, I trust you'll have the tact not to tell anyone of your involvement. Do you understand?"

"Perfectly," Nick said.

"And you'll take the part?"

"All right."

Judith smiled, then purred the question which she thought she already knew the answer to.

"And who would you like to play opposite you as Juliet?"

Nick looked from Ms Howard to Joyce Jones to Mike, almost as though he expected one of them to tell him the answer. Then he put his head in his hands. Why was he making a show of it? He must know that Mike knew he was going out with Rachel. The three teachers glanced at each other. Then Joyce and Judith were both looking to Mike for the next move.

"Are you all right, Nick?" he asked.

"Yes, sir," Nick muttered. "I'm making up my mind."

The three teachers sat there as the bell went for the end of break. Slowly, Nick raised his head.

"Well?" Judith said, her patience almost gone.

Nick took a deep breath. "Rachel," he said. "I'll play Romeo, as long as Rachel's Juliet."

As Mike and Phil were driving away from school that day, they passed Rachel and Becky, walking home.

"This'll only take a minute," Mike said, slowing down. He waved at Rachel and got out of the car. She looked pleased to see him.

"I thought I'd put you out of your suspense," he said. "You got the part."

Rachel looked like she wanted to kiss him. "That's wonderful," she said. "Oh, thank you, sir. That's brilliant!"

Mike was getting back into the car when she remembered to ask, "Who's Romeo?"

"Nick is."

Her face fell. Becky, too, looked annoyed.

"But Nick wasn't even at the auditions," Rachel complained. "I thought ..."

"What's wrong?"

"Never mind. Thank you, sir. See you tomorrow."

As Mike and Phil drove off, the two girls were already in deep discussion. It was surprising, but obvious: Rachel had finished with Nick. Now the lad wanted to use the part to get her back. That could cause problems in the play; Judith Howard would be fed up when she found out. But Mike wasn't.

"What's the good news?" Phil asked, as they turned on to Gregory Boulevard.

"Pardon?"

"You've got a smile on your face. First I've seen in a fortnight."

"Oh, it's nothing," Mike said. "Nothing at all."

Part Two

One

Term was over. Murky autumn had given way to crisp, clear skies in the approach to Christmas. Rachel was feeling good about the world. She had no school for two weeks, and, tonight, she was going dancing.

On her way back from Becky's, Rachel saw an unfamiliar car outside the house. Quietly opening the front door, she could hear Mum's voice in the kitchen.

"I know this sounds very callous now, but it will get easier. The wound might never heal, but scar tissue will grow over it ..."

Then another woman's voice, one which Rachel didn't recognize. "It's hard to explain what it's like without him. I still burst into tears five times a day. The children are being much more mature about it than I am, but I don't know how we're going to cope when it gets to Christmas. You see, I had no idea ..."

Rachel went upstairs. Another of Mum's friends' husbands had walked out on her. For as long as Rachel could remember, Mum had attracted these wounded birds, anxious to learn how to cope in a world without men. Mum, ten years after being ditched by Dad, talked convincingly about women not needing men, how they were only good for making babies. She meant it, too. Rachel didn't agree with her.

Did Rachel miss Nick? Not much. She still saw him every

weekday. He stared mournfully at her in lessons. She wished that he wasn't in the play next term. Maybe being in the play would force them to get on with each other. Nick would get over her. He would find someone else. And so would Rachel. But not yet. Only yesterday, Mark Kepper asked her out. Mark was good-looking, but had a real reputation as a user. Rachel turned him down without a second thought. Mum was right about one thing: having a man wasn't everything. Her own life came first.

Rachel wanted coffee. She heard the car outside leave, so went downstairs to the kitchen. But Mum's guest was still there. She was about Mum's age, and had clearly been crying. Rachel thought she recognized her, but didn't know where from. Mum spoke.

"This is my daughter, Rachel. Rachel, you remember Tina Scott?"

"Rachel. Of course," Tina said. "You came to Colin's funeral. He used to speak about you."

Rachel was stuck for words. "I was very . . . very . . ."

Mrs Scott squeezed her hand. "We all were. But Colin wouldn't have wanted us to grieve for ever. *Life goes on.* That's what he would have said. What's your new teacher like?"

"Nice," Rachel said, not sure if this was an insult to Mr Scott's memory. "But not very experienced. I'm sure he'll get us all through the exams, but I still – I still miss . . ."

She found herself crying. Then Mrs Scott was crying, too. Mum had to comfort them both.

When Mrs Scott finally left, Mum made herself and Rachel some strong coffee.

"You could have timed that better," she told Rachel. "I bumped into Tina at the shops, looking suicidal, so I dragged her back here. I'd just about calmed her down when you turned up."

"I'm sorry," Rachel said. "I didn't mean to break down like that."

"I know you were very fond of him," Mum said, comfortingly.

"I was," Rachel said, "but it wasn't only that. Mrs . . . Tina was right. Life does go on. Mr Scott's barely been dead for two months, but I haven't thought about him for weeks. Doesn't that make me awful?"

"No, that's silly. There's so much happening in your life that you have to leave things behind, keep moving on. There's no need to feel guilty."

Rachel stared into space.

"Where are you going tonight?" Mum asked, sitting down opposite her.

"Rock City. There's a bunch of us going to celebrate the end of term."

"All girls?" Mum murmured, as she stirred sweetener into her drink.

"Gary's giving us a lift."

"Just you be careful. I don't want you having too much to drink or trying some kind of drug and ending up in bed with a strange man."

"Mum, even if I wanted them, which I don't, I can't afford drugs or lots to drink," Rachel protested.

"You don't have to have the money," Mum lectured. "There are lots of men who'll give them to a good-looking girl like you."

Rachel groaned, though she knew her mother meant well. Rachel didn't enjoy getting drunk, not very drunk anyhow. Nor was she into drugs. She'd tried dope when she was going out with Carl in the summer, but it only gave her a head-ache. Carl said it was because she wasn't used to the tobacco he'd mixed it with.

"You have to trust me," was all she said to Mum now.

"I do trust you," Mum said. "I want you to have a good time, safely."

They left it at that.

Rock City wasn't like a lot of nightclubs, where people dressed to look as glamorous as possible. It was pretty casual, although if you wore a T-shirt with the wrong band name on it people wouldn't take you seriously. Rachel chose her T-shirt carefully and put on black Levis, then spent a lot of time making sure her hair and face were right. You had to be eighteen to get in and Rachel didn't want the guy on the door to give her a second glance.

Becky's boyfriend, Gary, drove them there and would take them home, too. Rachel was supposed to be staying at Dad's that weekend, but they'd agreed that she would go round for Sunday dinner and stay over until Monday instead.

Rock City was crowded. The girls got in without any trouble, arriving just before ten when the price went up. Carmen was with them, as was Carla Green, who was in Rachel and Becky's English group. Rachel wasn't terribly keen on Carla. She was a bit giggly, and very pally with Kate Duerden, who Rachel actively disliked. But she was all right in a group. Gary, squiring so many girls, seemed uncom-fortable. Once they were in, he and Becky headed straight for the bar.

The dance floor heaved. The girls danced to Rachel's favourite song. Oasis told Rachel that she was free to be whatever she wanted, and she wanted to believe them. Strobe-effect lights panned the heads of the crowd.

"So tell me," Carla asked Rachel, shouting over the throbbing music, "why did you split up with Nick?"

"Nick who?" Rachel said, not wanting to be drawn on the subject.

Carla smiled. "Yeah," she said. "Right."

A man with long, dark hair and a spangly waistcoat began to dance in front of Rachel. That was the way it worked. No one ever asked you to dance. They moved in and found out how you reacted. This bloke looked about thirty. Rachel gave him the cold shoulder. She wanted someone mature, but not as mature as that.

"I don't want to go," Mike told Phil. "Those places are meat markets."

"Rock City's not," Phil said. "People get buses from Leicester, Sheffield, Birmingham ... great atmosphere, great music. It's not just a pick-up joint."

"I still don't know."

"Come on, mate. It's Christmas. Get a life."

Mike finished his pint. Phil was right. The night was still young. He hadn't got out of bed until noon this morning. He didn't have to teach for a fortnight.

"Will they let me in, dressed like this?"

He was wearing a woollen waistcoat, a red T-shirt and faded jeans, torn at the knee.

"Sure. It's Saturday night. No dress code."

The two men queued for nearly half an hour to get in. By the time they'd checked their coats, Mike needed to dance just to warm himself up. While Phil went to get drinks, Mike made for the dance floor.

"Don't I know you?"

A well-built blonde woman was shouting at him. Mike shook his head shyly. The blonde gave him a cheeky smile. Then, when Mike didn't try to make conversation or even turn fully to her, she moved away. Mike felt foolish. She'd been trying to pick him up. He found her quite attractive, but he was out of practice. Actually, he'd never really been in practice. With him, women always made the running.

Mike had been single for a month, but wasn't used to it yet. Did you ever get used to it? He'd been with Emma for four years – less if you didn't count the early months before he and Emma were officially going out. During that time he'd had a few nothingy dates with other students. All they did was make him realize how much he wanted Emma. *Emma.* He wasn't over her yet. Phil said that what Mike needed was a few brief flings. But Mike had never had a one-night stand in his life. He wasn't spontaneous enough. He had never learned to seize the moment. Maybe it was time.

Phil returned with two beers and Mike had to stop dancing. There was nowhere safe to leave drinks. Dancing glass in hand required a better balancing act than Mike was capable of. They stood at the raised section by the entrance looking down on the dance floor. Phil pointed out a woman he fancied. She had a short, blonde bob and a dress that was little more than a long T-shirt. The girl was pretty, but rather young, Mike thought.

"What's your type?" Phil asked him.

"I don't have a type," Mike told him. "I never pick women. They pick me."

"Lucky you," Phil said.

It sounded impressive, Mike knew, unless you realized that he had only ever slept with two women: Vicky and

Emma. Mike tried to think positive. He felt more attractive now because, this morning, he'd shaved off his beard.

Mike had hated that beard. He'd only kept it for Emma, but Emma's opinion no longer mattered. Today, seeing himself without it, Mike felt more at ease, more ... innocent somehow. He felt like he'd spent the last year trying to pretend that he was older than he really was.

Phil was still drunkenly going on about what kind of women Mike fancied.

"Yeah, but if you *had* to choose," he insisted, "give me an example, c'mon. Madonna? Claudia Schiffer? Janet Jackson? Who?"

"I'd choose someone I've met," Mike complained, "not someone I've only seen in an airbrushed photograph."

"Who then?"

Mike tried to make female forms float across his imagination. For some reason, the only image which came to mind was that of Rachel Webster, from school. Forbidden fruit. He wasn't going to tell Phil that.

"The woman over there's attractive," he said, pointing at the blonde who'd tried to chat him up, earlier. This is the way desire works, he'd read somewhere. We are attracted to those who are attracted to us. If she hadn't talked to him earlier, would he have picked her?

"Like them older, do you?" Phil teased, downing his pint. "Follow me." He was right, Mike realized, as they got closer to her. She was at least thirty.

"My name's Phil," Phil shouted, gliding in front of her. "What's yours?"

"Evelyn," the woman shouted back.

"This is Mike," Phil shouted, pointing behind him. "He's shy. Dance with him, would you?"

A moment later, Phil was gone.

"Hi, Mike," Evelyn said. "We meet again."

They danced for twenty minutes. To Mike's relief, conversation was impossible. Then Evelyn had to go to the toilet and Mike offered to buy her a drink. Rock City had a few places where you could sit down and talk, though they were all very noisy. Evelyn returned, having reconstructed her make-up. They went upstairs, where it was easier to get served. Mike had a good view of the dance floor below. Phil was dancing next to the blonde bob. She was smiling a lot.

Evelyn didn't seem bothered that she couldn't hear half of what Mike said. She told him that she worked in a bookies. Mike was vague about his job, thinking it would put her off him. Conversation didn't matter tonight, anyway. When they kissed for the first time, it was weird. Without his beard, Mike felt naked.

"Relax," Evelyn said. "I'm not going to eat you."

When they kissed again, Mike realized that she would, without hesitation, go to bed with him that night. He began to relax. Maybe Phil was right and this was what he needed: an uncomplicated one-night stand.

They danced again. Phil was still dancing with the blonde, who he introduced as Tracey. The girl waved enthusiastically at Mike and Evelyn. Then, as Mike moved away, he noticed something which made him uncomfortable. There, watching from the edge of the dance floor, were three girls from school: Carla Green, a black girl who Mike recognized from school and – wouldn't you know it? – Rachel Webster. Seeing him see them, Carla waved and the three girls came over. Mike smiled bashfully at them. He was drunk, and didn't want to say anything he'd regret next term.

"Aren't you going to introduce us?" Carla asked, cheekily. Evelyn gave Mike a funny look.

"This is Evelyn," he yelled. "Evelyn, this is Carla, Rachel and ...?"

"Carmen," Carla said. "You know, you look a lot better without the beard."

Mike ignored the compliment and glanced directly at Rachel. She was dressed down, and, next to the fake glamour of the woman he was dancing with, looked very young. Rachel pointed at his chest.

"Snap," she said, with an embarrassed smile. He realized that they were wearing identical T-shirts.

"You've got good taste," he told her. "Merry Christmas, girls."

They were too young to be here, he thought, as the three girls found their own space on the dance floor. As a teacher, was he supposed to tell someone? It would feel hypocritical. He'd sneaked into pubs at their age. Mike watched the three girls as they joined Becky, who was dancing with a muscular bloke. Carla was pointing back towards the teachers and their partners.

"Let's go and have another drink," Mike suggested to Evelyn. He didn't enjoy dancing in a goldfish bowl.

"Your friend's not the only one who likes them young," Evelyn commented, loudly, as they climbed the stairs. "You had a thing with that girl in the T-shirt, didn't you? I could tell by the way you looked at her."

"No, no," Mike insisted.

In full view of the dance floor, Evelyn stopped and gave him a big kiss. That would give the girls something to talk about on the way home.

"Do you want to leave?" Evelyn asked.

Mike didn't have to think about it. "Why not?"

He hadn't bought any condoms yet, Mike realized, as they queued for their coats. He waved goodbye to Phil, then popped into one of the toilets. As he was returning to the foyer, he almost bumped into Rachel Webster. She gave him a bashful smile, but didn't speak. Evelyn had collected the coats already.

"Over here, Mike." She'd observed the encounter. "Doesn't say much, your friend, does she?"

Mike didn't feel like pretending. "She's not my friend, she's a pupil. I'm a school teacher."

Evelyn's expression changed from cynicism to sympathy. "I thought you wouldn't tell me about your job because you were on the dole."

"I was, until a few weeks ago," Mike told her. "Sometimes I think I preferred it."

They went out into the cold night air.

"I know you're meant to say your place or mine," Evelyn said, "but I've got a babysitter to pay off, so we'll go back to Carlton, if that's all right."

"Sure," Mike said.

Had she told him she had children? If so, he hadn't heard her.

"How many kids have you got?" he asked, politely.

"Just the one. He's seven. I divorced his dad two years ago."

They waited for a taxi to come. It was early, by night club standards, so at least there wasn't a large queue.

"There are usually loads outside," Evelyn said. "But this is what you get at Christmas, I suppose."

A cab pulled up and took the couple in front of them away. Evelyn checked her watch. It was ten to one. She had probably promised the sitter she'd be back by one, Mike realized. He wondered if she did this every week: picking up men to a deadline. Why shouldn't she? The club was full of blokes doing much the same.

Suddenly, to Mike's surprise, he couldn't go through with it. He hardly knew the woman standing next to him. In daylight, he probably wouldn't even fancy her. He didn't want to do the most intimate thing two people could do with a virtual stranger.

"I'm sorry," he told Evelyn. "I'm feeling ill. I'm going to have to go home."

She looked at him the way he looked at a child with a feeble excuse for forgetting his homework. "You're kidding," she said. "What's wrong? Is it me?"

"No, really. I've had a lot to drink and ..."

"It's the child, isn't it? You don't want to go near a woman who's got kids."

Mike found himself babbling. "No. Not at all. I promise. I've got this stomach ache and ..."

A taxi pulled up. "Come on then," Evelyn said. "I'd better drop you off. You're in Radford, aren't you? It's on the way."

"No, really," Mike told her. "I can walk. I'm sorry." He began to back away.

"I can walk," he repeated.

Evelyn gave him a look of disgust mingled with dismay. Mike turned on his heel and hurried up Talbot Street.

The walk home only took twenty minutes. Mike went straight to bed. He was still trying to sleep when he heard Phil come in. His landlord wasn't alone.

A few minutes later, Mike was kept awake by Phil and Tracey doing what he should have been doing with Evelyn.

Mike couldn't sleep. Had he done the right thing? Suddenly, sex with Evelyn had seemed the wrong thing to do. Yet, according to everything that Mike read and watched, the right thing no longer existed. Morality had nothing to do with anything, anywhere. People did what they wanted to do. People did whatever they could get away with.

He wondered whether Rachel Webster had got off with anybody that night.

Two

The spring term began with a tutor period, followed by an English lesson. Everyone wanted to talk about their Christmas. Rachel preferred not to. Her Christmas had been rubbish, as usual.

Rachel had spent only one Christmas Day with Dad since the divorce. That was three years ago, when Mum stayed with her sister in Preston. Rowan and Phoebe were very young then, and Rachel enjoyed playing with them. Still, the festival left a bitter flavour in her mouth. It gave Rachel a taste of what it would have been like to live in a real family, with real brothers and sisters, not a substitute step-family where the kids confused her with the babysitter.

Since then, Rachel had spent Christmas Day with Mum and various friends or visiting family members, then gone to her father's on Boxing Day. There was always an expensive present waiting for her in Mapperley Park. Dad tried to make Boxing Day a second Christmas Day. The fantasy never worked. This year, it fell particularly flat. Phoebe and Rowan were more interested in their new videos and computer games than in Rachel. There was constant tension between Dad and Clarissa. Twice, Rachel walked into a room to find them suddenly go silent.

Rachel wondered if one of them was having an affair. Dad was past it, she thought, but Clarissa wasn't. After all, the children were both at school now. Clarissa was still attractive. She didn't have a job, though she did voluntary work for Citizen's Advice now and then. It would hardly be surprising if Clarissa had a fling to fill her empty days. Rachel thought that it would serve Dad right, for what he did to Mum. But Rachel hoped they wouldn't split up. It wasn't fair, when children were involved. Rachel had long since lost her illusions about Dad returning to Mum.

Rachel would never admit it to her friends, but she was glad to be back at school. Over the holiday, she had read and reread the part of Juliet. Once the mock exams were over, the play rehearsals began in earnest.

Today, the class reached Act Four. Mr Steadman talked the group through difficult bits of vocabulary, making sure the plot was clear. He looked much nicer without his beard, Rachel thought, barely old enough to be a teacher. That night at Rock City, she had taken him for a teenager, wearing the same T-shirt as her. For a fleeting moment, she'd fancied him. Then Carla pointed out who he was. Now Steadman was coming to the end of the lesson. There was some whispering and giggling from behind Rachel. The teacher started to get irritated.

"Come on, everyone. There're only five minutes of the lesson left. Let's see if we can keep concentrating." He paused, seeing something. "What is that?"

"Nothing, sir," Kate Duerden said, unconvincingly.

Rachel glanced back. She couldn't believe it. Lisa and Kate were passing notes around, like little girls at junior school. As Steadman walked over, Kate thrust the note to Rachel, expecting her to hide it. Rachel did nothing of the kind. She glanced at the note, a page torn from an exercise book. It was a scribbled conversation between Kate and Carla. Rachel only read the middle of it.

You should have seen the girl Hansen got off with! She looked younger than me! Carla had written.

What about Steadman's? Kate wrote back.

His looked older than my mother! Carla replied. *She was all over him.*

"I'll take that, Rachel." Before Rachel could read any further, the English teacher snatched the note away from her. She blushed. When she looked up at the teacher, he was reading the note and turning red himself.

"Rachel, stay behind," he ordered.

"Sorry," Kate whispered, as the lesson ended. "I owe you."

Carla avoided Rachel's eyes as she walked out. Rachel told Becky what she'd been doing.

"That's the last time she goes clubbing with us," Becky whispered. "Still, it gets you and Steadman alone together. You know, I think he likes you."

"Oh, sure," Rachel said, loading on the sarcasm as Becky left the room.

"Who wrote this?" Mr Steadman asked, when they were alone in the room together. He looked angry.

"It wasn't me," Rachel said.

"I know that," Steadman told her. "I know your writing. This looks more like Carla – and Kate. Am I right?"

There was no point in denying it.

"I had nothing to do with the note," Rachel said.

"Except you were reading it."

"There was nothing there that I didn't know already."

Mr Steadman sat on his desk and leant forward. "Look," he said. "The people who ought to be embarrassed are you and your friends. Mr Hansen and I are old enough to go to Rock City. You aren't. But we didn't say anything, which could get us into trouble. Now I get . . . this. Next time, I think I'd better report you to the management, have you thrown out."

Embarrassed, Rachel tried to apologize. "I wasn't spreading gossip. I don't want to fall out with you, sir. You helped me get the part in the play and I'm very grateful."

Steadman sighed. "I suppose I kept the wrong girl behind," he said.

He got up to go, but seemed in no hurry. "Did you have a good time?" he asked. "Christmas and all that?"

Rachel shrugged. "Rock City was all right. Christmas was pretty awful, as usual." She could have left then, but found herself lingering. "How about you?" she asked.

"Not much better than yours, I suspect." He frowned, then added, "My parents divorced while I was at university. Going home isn't much fun."

"Mine split up when I was five," Rachel told him.

He smiled sympathetically.

"Your friend seemed nice," Rachel said, trying to be cheerful. "Evelyn. Are you still seeing her?"

Steadman shook his head with a wry smile.

"On that point, at least, Carla was right," he said. "She was a little too old for me."

"They say age is all in the mind," Rachel told him.

"In that case," Steadman replied, with a boyish grin, "you're probably older than I am. I still feel about fourteen half the time."

Rachel wanted to tell him that part of her seemed permanently stuck at twelve. The better part. But then the bell went for the end of break. Steadman opened the door and they both hurried to their next lessons.

At home that night, Mum was playing old records. She had

everything by the Beatles, who were cool again at the moment. John, Paul and George were asking Rachel whether she believed in love at first sight. She didn't. For some people – the Romeos and Juliets of this world – it might happen all the time. Not Rachel. She knew that for her, if she was lucky, love would come more slowly, like a cut flower which steadily swelled until it reached full bloom. Though not all flowers opened fully. Some wilted and withered before they'd opened at all.

It was the second weekend of term and Rachel was surprised to find herself with feelings for someone new.

"Penny for them," Mum said.

"Oh, it's nothing," Rachel told her.

Sometimes Rachel felt like her mum could read her mind, and it was comforting. Today, though, Rachel didn't want Mum to know her secret thoughts.

"Are you disappointed about not seeing your father?" Mum asked.

Dad had cancelled her visit this weekend at short notice. "Something came up" was all he said by way of explanation. Rachel shook her head. "Hardly," she said, "except that it leaves me with nothing to do. Becky's out with Gary. Carmen's got a boyfriend now, too."

"That's the trouble with girl gangs," Mum said. "If you're not careful, as soon as boys become important, old loyalties get swept aside. But maybe you're sorry about dropping Nick. You could call him, you know."

"Definitely not," Rachel said. "I'll be seeing enough of him once the play rehearsals start on Tuesday."

"You could come to the pictures with Janice and me. We're going to see that film that's on at Broadway."

"It's all right," Rachel said, "I don't like films with

subtitles. I'll stay home and revise."

"Suit yourself," Mum said. "But it is Saturday night."

When Mum went out for the evening, Rachel read her science textbook for a few minutes, then ran herself a bath. She put some bubble bath in, and while the bath ran, looked at her naked body in the mirror. She was trying to decide what an older man would think of it. She was a bit skinny. But some men liked skinny girls. Rachel wondered if her new English teacher was one of them.

As steam misted the mirror, Rachel got into the bath. She wondered what sex would be like. Becky was always surprisingly coy on the subject. With one hand beneath the bubbles, Rachel imagined what it would be like with Mike (that was his first name – Rachel had heard Evelyn use it). None of her friends knew that she found him attractive. Oh, Becky had made a couple of jokes about the teacher keeping Rachel behind. She thought that Steadman had a thing about *her*. Rachel wasn't so sure. She liked the way Mike talked to her today, like she was an adult. She caught him looking at her sometimes, too. But it was probably her imagination.

Rachel would never go out with the English teacher, she recognized that, even as her head flooded with feeling. This was only a fantasy, something to keep her going through cold, boring January. Steadman was too old and too straight to contemplate a relationship with a girl her age, even if Becky was right and he did fancy her. But it was fun to fantasize about Mike, her forbidden lover. Daydreams would have to keep her going until summer, when the exams were over, and she had time to look for the real thing.

Three

Something happened to Mike's teaching in the spring term at Stonywood. He began to enjoy it more. He no longer started some days filled with terror at the prospect of all the things which might go wrong. He still finished each day exhausted, especially when there was a play rehearsal, and needed to sleep as soon as he got home. But at least Phil was there. Unlike Emma, Phil understood the pressures of teaching. They could share stories about nightmare lessons. And the really bad days were now few and far between. Mike even found himself looking forward to some lessons – his year seven for instance, where Paul Wilks had just written a story which was a whole page long – and he no longer dreaded parents' evenings.

Year-eleven parents' evening was the big one. Since Mike had a top group, nearly every parent would be attending. His subject was worth two separate GCSE grades – Language and Literature – to each student. Naturally, therefore, the parents were anxious for their child to do well. Many questioned Mike closely.

Some teachers hated parents' evenings, but the more committed ones seemed to enjoy them. Mike began to understand why. Now and then, to his surprise, the parents told him how much their kids enjoyed his lessons.

"We were a bit worried when Mr Scott died so suddenly, but our Matthew says you work them really hard. We were pleased with his mock exam results."

A few parents brought their child with them. Kate Duerden squirmed by her mother's side while Mike read the Riot Act.

"She's perfectly capable of getting a C if she puts her back into it, but her concentration is poor and she often distracts others. She needs to grow up." The working-class parents, Mike was beginning to realize, appreciated plain speaking. The more middle-class ones preferred him to sound academic. For Nick Cowan's parents, he gave a detailed analysis of the skills which Nick excelled at, then highlighted those where there was room for improvement.

"His use of quotations is slapdash. He knows his stuff, but assumes that the reader knows he knows, which won't do in an exam. His punctuation is still haphazard, too. Shakespeare could get away with changing the rules whenever he felt like it, but he didn't have to sit GCSE English."

Guiltily, Mike reassured Nick's parents that his being in the play wouldn't interfere with his exam preparation. "The mocks show him well on course for two As. Being in the play will help him with *Romeo and Juliet*."

"Some of his other teachers are worried about the time he's already putting into the play," Mrs Cowan said. "Take his maths, for instance. He's never been terribly good at maths, but he needs to get a C to go to university."

"I'm sure he'll be all right," Mike told her, lamely.

The most intriguing meeting of the evening was with Rachel Webster's parents. Mike knew that they were divorced, but they turned up together towards the end, when he was getting very tired. The father was a thin, intense man with a receding hair line and an arrogant glint in his eye. He quickly let Mike know that he was a university lecturer, slipping it into the conversation in a casual but calculated way. He praised Mike's teaching, but it was easy to see that he wasn't sincere. Like many upwardly mobile, middle-class parents, this one wanted special treatment for his own child. The mother seemed embarrassed.

Rachel, as it happened, was already getting special treatment from Mike. He spent longer marking her work than he did that of other students, and took every opportunity he got to talk to her. They had a warm, easy relationship. Mike was sure that Rachel thought he was only being friendly. The truth was, he had a bit of a crush on the girl. Some nights, unable to sleep, he manufactured a fantasy where, forced together by circumstance, the two of them ended up together.

But it was only make-believe. Probably most teachers his age had similar feelings. They were only human. And Mike would no more make a pass at Rachel Webster than he would at the year-eight girl who was always staring at him, moon-eyed, during reading lessons. Mike tried to keep these thoughts far from his mind as he rambled on about what a good student Rachel was.

Finally, Rachel's mother managed to get a word in edgeways. She, too, praised Mike for the way he'd taken over the class. But she was worried about the time that being in the play would take away from Rachel's other subjects.

"Rachel's not all that academic. She struggles with languages and her maths is very borderline, Mr Hansen says."

Mike promised to have a word with Mr Hansen. He'd do it tonight, if Phil didn't want dropping off at Tracey's, which happened more and more often these days.

Mike tried to talk calmly to Rachel's mother, but had

trouble concentrating. He kept seeing traces of Rachel in the woman's face.

"I'm sorry," he told her, after a while. "I'm repeating myself. It's been a long day."

"We understand," Mr Webster said.

There was a queue of parents waiting. Mike's appointment system was way out of kilter. He shook hands and said goodbye. No sooner were they gone than another couple took their place.

"Mr and Mrs Guest. Good to see you ..."

Mike ran way over. When he finished, there was only the Head of Year and one of the Deputy Heads left. Phil must have got a lift with somebody else. There was a drink on in a local pub, but Mike had had enough of talking about teaching for one day. He was heading for the car park when he bumped into Sarah Poole. Sarah was a geography teacher a couple of years older than him. She was also his Union representative, so he'd talked to her, briefly, a couple of times.

"You look as tired as I feel," she said. "Phil asked me to tell you he'd gone for the bus. An hour ago."

"I don't blame him," Mike told her. "Why're you still here?"

"I've got a year-eleven tutor group as well as the group I teach," she told him. "This evening has taken for ever." Then she added. "You look like you need a drink. Come across the road. I'll buy you one."

Why not? Mike thought. He was too tired to drive. Too tired even to think.

Mike was afraid that Sarah would tell him off for not attending Union meetings, but she seemed more interested in finding out how he was getting on.

"It was a nightmare the first few weeks," he told her, "commuting from Sheffield, but I'm sharing a house with Phil Hansen now."

"Why'd it take you so long to move?" Sarah enquired.

To Mike's surprise, he found himself explaining about Emma. He was too tired to be concise, and the explanation took longer than it should have. Sarah listened patiently.

"You never saw it coming?" she asked, when he'd finished.

"Not for a moment."

"It's rotten," Sarah told him, putting her hand over his in sympathy. "It happened to me last year. We'd been together since university."

"I'm sorry."

"He met someone else, at work. I had no idea. He told me on the last day of the summer term: *it's over, I'm leaving you, bye*. I'm only starting to get over it now."

Mike didn't know what to say to that. This was the first sustained conversation he'd had with Sarah. Yet here they were, exchanging intimate secrets like a Lonely Hearts Club. After a couple of silent minutes they finished their drinks. As they were getting up to go, Sarah wrote something down on a beer mat.

"This is my new phone number," she told him. "If you want to do this again some time, don't talk to me at school, call me. OK?"

"OK," Mike said. "I'll do that."

He drove home slowly, thinking about Sarah. She was nice. He would appreciate her friendship. Aside from Phil and people he talked to in passing at his local, Mike had no friends in Nottingham. But maybe Sarah was interested in more than friendship. Mike wasn't sure if it was a good idea, going out with someone you worked with. Not only that, but, with her strong features and long black hair, Sarah reminded him of his first girlfriend, Vicky. He could do without that.

Mike stopped at some lights. The thought of resemblances took him back to Rachel Webster and her mother. Most women turned into their mothers, so it was said. If so, Rachel's wasn't bad. A little tired-looking, perhaps, but ... There was a honk behind him, and Mike snapped to attention, realizing that the lights had turned green.

Four

There were only three people left in the drama studio when Nick kissed Rachel. It was a brief kiss, not as soft as the ones they'd shared before Christmas. Then he spoke, softly, "*Thus from my lips, by thine, my sin is purged.*"

Rachel replied, "*Then have my lips the sin that they have took.*"

Nick gave her his familiar, mischievous smile.

"*Sin from my lips? O trespass sweetly urged! Give me my sin again.*"

The next kiss was longer. "*You kiss by the book,*" Rachel told him. Then she turned and spoke to Mr Steadman. "What am I supposed to mean there?"

"You're teasing him," the teacher said. "Saying that he's learnt how to kiss from a manual."

"But how would I know?" Rachel asked. "I'm not even fourteen yet. I've probably never kissed a boy, whereas Romeo's at least eighteen ..."

"Isn't that what young lovers do?" Steadman suggested, lightly. "Don't they like to pretend to be more experienced than they are?"

"I suppose so," Rachel agreed, after a little thought. "Are we going to do the bit where the nurse comes in?"

"Can't," Steadman told her. "Maxine's gone home. And the next section's crucial. We should do it when we're all more awake. Why don't we run through that last page one more time?"

Rachel and Nick kissed again, and again. Was this why he'd wanted the part? Rachel wondered. Did Nick think that acting the part of lovers might change Rachel's feelings for him? If so, it wouldn't work. This wasn't a real kiss. This was acting. When they kissed, the kiss might taste the same as when they went out with each other. But Nick wasn't Nick. He was Romeo. Nick ought to understand that.

Outside, it was raining heavily.

"I'll give you two a lift home," Mr Steadman said.

Nick looked disappointed. He had an umbrella, Rachel saw. He'd been hoping to walk her home alone. There weren't many rehearsals where it ended up with just the two of them, together. Rachel felt grateful to the teacher.

She and Nick got into the back seat of Mr Steadman's Escort. Nick's house was nearer and they went there first. Mr Steadman drove in silence. He seemed tired. Rachel and Nick sat apart, with Rachel's bag between them, not saying a word to each other. Rachel wished that she was sitting in the front, next to Mike Steadman. Nick gave directions to his house, then thanked the teacher politely as he got out.

"Can I move to the front seat?" Rachel asked, as Nick hurried up the path to his front door in the rain. "I can see where we're going better."

"Sure."

He opened the door. Rachel hopped out and back in again, tucking her bag beneath her feet. She hoped that Nick hadn't noticed what she was doing. Back in the car, she fumbled with the seatbelt. The teacher leant over and pulled the buckle out for her. Rachel felt the warmth of his body press against hers.

"You'd better tell me where to go," he said, moving into

first gear. Rachel gave him directions. Mr Steadman drove slowly in the teeming rain. Rachel wanted to make conversation but wasn't sure what to say. She had been alone with Mike Steadman before, but never so intimately.

"Left here?"

"Yes."

The teacher kept his eyes on the road, but Rachel saw him frown. She hoped he hadn't realized that she was taking him the long way home.

"You did well today," he told her.

"Thanks," Rachel said. "It's a bit odd, kissing someone again and again like that."

"You'll get used to it," Mike said, his voice becoming awkward. "But I can see it could be embarrassing, if you and Nick are ... finished."

"We never really started," Rachel told him, a little dishonestly. "That was Kate, mouthing off."

They'd reached her road.

"Turn in here," she said, sorry that the conversation, which was just getting going, had to end. Yet, as he parked, the teacher seemed in no hurry to leave.

"What do you do now?" Rachel asked. "Go home and spend the evening marking books, like Ken Barlow in *Coronation Street*?"

"Not tonight," Mike said. "Mr Hansen and I are driving to Leicester. We're going to see Suede."

Rachel was jealous. "I love them," she told him. "I wish I was going."

Mike turned and gave Rachel a fleeting look which seemed to say that he wished she was coming with him, too. Rachel smiled. She opened her mouth to make conversation about other groups. Carmen and Becky weren't into the music she liked. But she didn't speak because, suddenly, she was too nervous. In her fantasies, this would be the point where the teacher made a move.

She moved closer to him, reaching to unfasten her seat-belt, quivering like a fish out of water. His face was inches away from hers.

"I meant what I said," he told her, "about the acting. I know you're not as experienced as Nick and you lack confidence sometimes, but you're coming on. Today, you were really good."

"You were good too," Rachel said, shyly. "Thanks for everything."

Then, before she had the chance to think about it, before he had the time to turn away, Rachel leant forward and kissed him on the lips. It was a soft, quick kiss. In her day-dreams, this was all she needed to do. The next moment he swept her into his arms and they were tearing each other's clothes off. Now, in real life, the teacher stared at her, looking scared. Rachel was suddenly embarrassed.

"Goodnight, sir," she said, grabbing her bag from the floor, then opening the door to the wind and rain. "Thanks for the lift."

Rachel stood in the dark road, watching as his car drove off, letting herself be pelted by the heavy rain. She had an awful feeling that she'd blown it, that the teacher would never let her get that close to him again.

Five

During Wednesday morning's lesson, Mike avoided looking at Rachel. He was afraid that his face would betray him in some way. Afterwards, though, when the class had gone off to lunch, he thought about her. He'd been thinking about her on and off since she kissed him the night before. He couldn't decide whether ...

"Still here?" The door had opened without him hearing and Rachel had come back into the room. "I meant to ask," she said, her voice not quite natural, "what was the concert like, sir?"

Mike tried to smile and began clearing away.

"Pretty good," he said.

"What did they play?"

Mike stumbled over his reply. He described the films that the group used as a backdrop. He didn't say that one of the films showed a teenage girl who reminded him of her. He didn't say how he'd spent a lot of the show trying to sort out his feelings for the teenage girl standing in front of him now.

"Sounds brilliant," she said. "Are you going to anything else?"

"Not for a while. You?"

She shook her head, but lingered, as though she was about to say something else. "I'd better go and eat my lunch then," she said. "Bye."

"Bye, Rachel."

He'd thought, for a second, that she was going to say something about kissing him last night. Mike kept going over that kiss in his head, again and again. He wondered if Rachel was doing the same. That moment, when her lips met his, he had frozen. Did she understand the fear, the blind panic which didn't allow him to kiss her back the way he wanted to? Or did she take it as a rebuff?

Unless he'd got it all wrong. What if her kiss was only meant as a friendly peck – a thank you for a lift home? If he had responded the way he wished he had, Rachel would have been embarrassed. The story would have been all over school by the next day. Yet Mike didn't think so. Rachel was too mature. But she was only sixteen, he had to remind himself: a girl one minute, a woman the next.

Which one had kissed him?

"I hardly see you out of school these days," Carmen told Rachel, in maths on Friday.

"I thought you were spending most of your time with Darren," Rachel said. He was a boy who Carmen had started going out with over Christmas.

"I chucked him at the weekend," Carmen told her. "He was only interested in one thing."

Rachel lowered her voice. "Did you give it to him?"

Carmen smiled enigmatically. Her smile implied that she and Rachel were close, but not *that* close. Rachel was hurt. They might have drifted apart a bit recently, but she'd always told Carmen everything. Carmen looked around. No one was listening to them.

"Twice," she said. "Actually, I don't think he was very good at it."

"They say it takes practice," Rachel quipped.

"Well, he can find someone else to practise on."

They both laughed. "How about you and Nick?" Carmen asked. "Did you ever ...?"

"No!" Rachel protested, as though the idea were unthinkable.

"How is it, working with him on the play?"

"All right," Rachel said. "No, that's not true. It's a bit funny at times, but we deal with it. Romeo and Juliet aren't on stage together all that much."

"Any chance of you two getting back together?"

Rachel shook her head. "I think he's over it now."

Carmen laughed. "You don't see the way he looks at you."

"Still?"

"Still. I'm telling you, Rachel, he's got it bad."

Rachel buried her head in her hands. "I don't want to hear this."

Carmen whispered, "I'm sure you don't. But why do you think that he's in the play? He does loads of acting, but he's never been in a school play before. It's because of you."

Rachel swivelled her head round sharply. Carmen was right. Nick, at the other end of the room, *was* staring at her. His face went red and he pretended to return to work.

"So," Carmen said, "if you're not interested in Nick, who *are* you interested in?"

Rachel put on a silly, *luvvie* sort of voice. "There are more important things than men," she said. "I am an ac-*tress*. While I'm working on a play, I am devoted only to my art."

"Oh, all right," said Carmen, returning to her work, "don't tell me then."

Rachel was trying to figure out an opportunity to see Mike Steadman on his own again. She'd nearly bottled it, but eventually worked up the nerve to go back after Wednesday's lesson, ask him about the concert. And he'd been nice to her. However there hadn't been a chance since then. On Thursday, the rehearsal finished early. It was still light and the weather was good, so there was no chance of a lift home. In today's lesson, the teacher went over the Mock exam papers. Rachel had done well in the exam: not quite scraping an A, but near enough. When she called for help, Mike stood closer to her than was strictly necessary. Her query was trivial, but he answered it in a lot of detail. Their eyes kept meeting. They were both stringing the conversation out so it would last as long as possible. Rachel didn't think that she was imagining it any more.

There was no way that Rachel was going to tell Carmen any of this. Rachel would be opening herself to ridicule. Also, Carmen was a woman now, while Rachel was still a virgin. Her friend would think that she'd become a fantasizer like Lisa Sharpe, who'd had a crush on Mr Hansen all last term. The crush only ended when it became common knowledge that Mr Hansen had a girlfriend, who was a friend of a friend of someone's elder sister. Tracey was eighteen and worked as a dental receptionist, or so the gossip went. Rachel worried: maybe Mike Steadman had a girlfriend. Even worse, suppose he lived with someone?

This is where daydreams lead you, she told herself. *You fantasize about getting off with someone and end up half-believing it. I got away with the kiss, but if I really made a play for him, it'd be awful and embarrassing and I'd never be able to look him in the eye again.*

Still, Rachel couldn't stop herself figuring out ways she could get to see the teacher on his own. What harm was there in it?

Six

On Wednesday, Mike had a free period before his year-eleven group arrived. He was sitting in his classroom, reading up for the next lesson, when Rachel arrived early. Her face was animated. A week and a day had passed since she had kissed him goodnight. Mike had nearly convinced himself that, whatever his fantasies, her kiss had been meant as a polite peck. The girl liked him and he liked her: it was a normal teacher/student relationship. Now he gave her a relaxed smile. Seeing Rachel made him feel more alive. She was letting her hair grow for the play. It suited her.

"Hi, Rachel," Mike said, casually. "How're things?"

Rachel perched on the edge of his desk, her long, black-stockinged legs at a right angle to him.

"I'm a bit nervous about tomorrow's rehearsal, sir," she said. "There're so many lines. I'm not even sure about what half of them mean most of the time."

"You needn't worry," Mike assured her.

He hesitated. Rachel was breathing heavily. Mike tried to remind himself that she was just a child. But she wasn't.

"If you like," he added, "I could go over the speeches with you after school tonight."

"Could you?" Rachel jumped off the desk and straightened her skirt. "Here? That'd be brilliant."

The rest of the class began to arrive.

In the staffroom, at break, Mike told Phil that he'd have to take the bus home.

"I've got some work to prepare in school," Phil said. "I don't mind hanging around until your rehearsal's over."

"I really don't know how long it'll take," Mike told him. "Could be ages. You'd be better off getting a lift from someone else, or the bus."

Phil gave Mike a peculiar look, but it wasn't his car. He couldn't argue.

The afternoon lasted for ever. Mike was too distracted to teach properly, and the kids ran him ragged. Next week, Ms Howard was doing one of her "mentor" lesson observations. He'd have to do better if he wanted the option of keeping his job for another year.

When school was over, Mike waited anxiously for Rachel. His classroom had big red curtains. They blocked the sun which streamed in during the mornings. Mike closed them so that he and Rachel would have some privacy. Then he panicked and half opened them again, in case it looked suspicious. He put the chairs on top of tables, something he always forgot to get the kids to do. Then he took two down again and put them in a shaded corner where no one would be able to see them straight away, not even if they opened the door.

Next, Mike picked up a few bits of rubbish from the floor. His classroom was noticeably less messy at the end of the day than it had been last term. Even so, there were still more sweet wrappers, balls of paper and discarded particles of pen than you saw in most classrooms. He didn't want Rachel to notice. Finally, Mike put the bins outside. The cleaner would recognize this as a message that there was a meeting going on and he shouldn't come in.

Rachel was late. Perhaps she'd had second thoughts. All of this could be totally innocent, Mike reminded himself. But what if it wasn't? He had no idea what to do. Making a move here would be like playing with fire. Best to wait until he gave her a lift home, and he was parking outside her house. But what if they were seen there? Oh, he must stop doing this. It wasn't real. It was ...

"Hi, sir," Rachel said, slipping quietly into the room. "This is really good of you."

"No problem," Mike said.

He saw at a glance why she had taken her time. She'd been making herself up. Her hair was carefully brushed and she was wearing blusher. He hadn't read the signals wrongly. He really ought to stop this now. Rachel smiled nervously and Mike began to sweat.

"Please," he said. "Sit down."

Rachel took the seat which Mr Steadman offered her. The teacher looked edgy. He'd taken his tie off. He had a copy of the play by his side but made no effort to open it. The school was quiet. Last lesson was long over. Most people were gone. Mr Steadman stared at her, the same frightened expression in his eyes that he'd had the week before, when Rachel kissed him. She knew that he knew.

But this wasn't real yet. This was the game she and Becky used to play when they were kids, at the swimming pool. They'd stand on the high diving board, daring each other to get closer and closer to the edge. There was always the risk that one would push the other and she would topple into the deep end. But it never happened. What usually happened was that an attendant came along, and told them to get off there before he threw them out.

Then, one day, the deep end no longer seemed so scary. First Becky, then Rachel, dived in, and swam. It was no longer a game. Now Rachel stared at the deep blue pool from the top of the diving-board ladder.

"I can understand you being nervous," Mr Steadman said, opening the book. "This is a demanding scene. And a lot of the lines are so well known that it's hard to take them seriously any more."

"I know," said Rachel. "It's a bit ... intimidating."

"Why don't we read it through," the teacher suggested. "At first, you're reacting while Romeo stands beneath the balcony. I don't think Ms Howard's decided how to stage that yet. Your first words are *Ay me*. How do you want to say them?"

"In a longing voice," Rachel said. "She's not sure whether he's there or not."

"Fine," the teacher said. "Say it."

Her chest quivering, Rachel breathed the words. Mr Steadman read Romeo's lines. His voice was totally unlike Nick's. It was assured, poetic, powerful. When he'd finished, Rachel paused.

"Come on," the teacher said. "We're alone. Go for it."

Rachel read the dreaded words:

"O Romeo, Romeo! wherefore art thou Romeo?
Deny thy father and refuse thy name.
Or, if thou wilt not, be but sworn my love,
And I'll no longer be a Capulet."

"That was fine," Mr Steadman said. "You sounded excited and earnest."

Their eyes met.

"Let's carry on," the teacher said.

There was a banging noise outside. Rachel and Mike glanced at the door, as though they'd been caught in some clandestine act. But no one came in. If they had, all they would see would be teacher and pupil sitting unusually close together. Rachel read. The words in the scene seemed to set their own pace.

Rachel read them faster and faster. Mike leant forward. "Slow down a little. You've got to give the audience time to enjoy the lines. Let them breathe."

"It's hard."

"Yes. The scene's very urgent, very serious. But it's also very ..." He paused and took a breath before completing the sentence. "Very sexy."

"I know what you mean," Rachel said. "Where shall I take it from?"

"After *do not swear*."

Rachel read more slowly:

"Although I joy in thee,
I have no joy of this contract tonight.
It is too rash, too unadvised, too sudden;
Too like the lightning, which doth cease to be
Ere one can say 'It lightens'. Sweet, good night!
This bud of love, by summer's ripening breath,
May prove a beauteous flower when next we meet.
Good night, good night! As sweet repose and rest
Come to thy heart as that within my breast!"

Mr Steadman read Romeo softly, slowly moving his chair nearer to hers. "*O, wilt thou leave me so unsatisfied?*"

Rachel replied, lifting her head so that their eyes met. "*What satisfaction canst thou have tonight?*"

But, before Mr Steadman could reply, she corpsed. The tension was too much for Rachel. Mr Steadman laughed too. Then there was an awkward silence.

"It feels like we're flirting with each other," he said, in a careful voice.

His face was inches from hers. Rachel could feel the heat of his breath on her forehead. She wanted to reach over and touch him.

"Are we?" she asked.

Neither of them was smiling now. They stared into each other's eyes. "This is very dangerous," Mr Steadman said, his head tilting towards hers.

They kissed.

At first it was a soft, gentle kiss, but it quickly became more. Mike's arms reached around her waist and he pulled her to him. Their lips parted for a moment as Rachel slid out of her chair on to his lap. Their tongues met hungrily. Her breasts swelled against his chest. Rachel slipped her hands inside the teacher's shirt, gripping the teacher's back as he lifted and pressed her closer to him. At that moment, the only thing she wanted in the world was to make love with him, there, and then. She would die happy.

There was a clattering outside and they broke apart like frightened animals.

"Let's get out of here," the teacher said.

Rachel said nothing. She adjusted her blouse, put her coat back on, and picked up her bag. Mike slid on his jacket, then pushed the door open a few inches.

"It's all right," he whispered to Rachel. "The cleaner's in the next room. Let's go out the side way."

They hurried down the corridor into the car park. It was five past four and the sun was only just beginning to set. Several cars remained in the car park, Mike's being the oldest one. He got in and opened the passenger door. Rachel tried to remain calm, to look as though it was the most normal thing in the world for a young male teacher to be giving a lone female pupil a lift home. Inside, though,

Rachel's body was shaking with excitement. Mike started the car, stalled it, then they raced out into the busy main road.

"Is there somewhere quiet we can go?" Mr Steadman asked.

"Your place?" Rachel whispered.

He shook his head. "I share a house with Phil Hansen. He'll be there."

"My mum's not home yet," Rachel said. "But there are kids from school on our street. Someone might ..."

"Isn't there somewhere we can just park? I don't know the city very well yet. The Forest, maybe ..."

"No," Rachel said. "I know a place. Get on to Mansfield Road."

They skirted round the ringroad.

"It's a car park," Rachel said. "Never very busy. Left here, then it's a right turn just after the brow of the hill."

They turned into the car park. Mike stopped the car in a corner, away from the other vehicles. Then they kissed again, as hungrily as before, despite their cramped conditions. "This is insane," Mike said, as their lips parted. "What are we doing?"

"We're doing what we've been waiting to do," Rachel told him. She gripped his hand. He couldn't back out now, not when they'd only just started. They kissed again, for several minutes this time, their hands exploring each others' bodies.

"What is this place?" Mike asked, when they finally broke apart.

"A park. Quite a big one."

"Can we go for a walk? Is it safe?"

"I think so," Rachel told him. "We're far enough from school."

They walked up a hill into the park itself, self-consciously holding hands but saying nothing. Rachel knew this park well. Today, though, she felt like she was seeing it for the first time. To their right was Woodthorpe Grange. To the left there were some small, formal gardens. In front of the couple was an expanse of grass, with a pitch-and-putt on one side and a tiny play area on the other.

Rachel used to come here all the time with her father, when she was six. That was just after he and Mum first separated. Dad couldn't think of anywhere else to take her. They'd walk. He'd try to talk to her. Eventually, he'd give up and they'd go to the little playground down the hill.

This afternoon, the place was nearly empty. Beyond the park's trees, the city's suburbs spread out before them. Two tall blocks of flats both broke the picture and gave it perspective. A deep red sun was setting over Nottingham. Blood-coloured blotches stained the clouds.

They turned away from the wide open spaces and walked back to the gardens. There were gaps in the hedge which bordered them. The couple eased through one into a secluded area of scrub which backed on to some houses. They were almost hidden. Without speaking, they embraced again, and again, and again.

"We've got to keep this so secret," Mike told her.

"I know," Rachel assured him.

"I don't even know where we can meet."

"We'll find a way."

"I'm crazy about you," Mike said. "You know that, don't you?"

Rachel planted a soft, chaste kiss on his lips. "I do now."

The sun was nearly gone and a cold wind was getting up.

Rachel checked her watch. "I'd better go," she said. "If I'm not in when Mum gets home, she worries."

They walked slowly back to the car, huddling up to each other. Mike drove back. This time, Rachel directed Mike the quick way to her house. They parked round the corner, on a side street. Mike got a piece of paper out of his jacket and wrote his address and phone number on it.

"Phil often goes out in the evening, to his girlfriend's. Sometimes he stays the night. He's usually gone by eight, if he's going." He hesitated. "The phone's not private. If I pick it up and say 'wrong number', you'll know he's in and I can't talk. If he answers, hang up."

"And what if you're free?" Rachel asked.

"Make some excuse to get out of the house. I'll collect you. We can go back to my place."

"I don't know," Rachel said, her mind still reeling from how quickly this was happening. "It's hard for me to go out late unless Mum knows where I'm going in advance. Can't you find out when Mr Hansen's definitely going to be out?"

"I can," Mike said. "But it might be a few days. I can't wait that long."

"Me neither," Rachel said.

Mike's hand crossed the gear stick and squeezed her leg. He was breathing heavily. Rachel steeled herself. She had dived into the deep end and now she was coming up for air. She unhooked the seatbelt and opened the door. Mike gave her a smile which he probably meant to be reassuring.

"We'll work it out," he said.

She gave him a glowing smile and he drove off, at speed. Rachel turned the corner and let herself into the empty house, her heart leaping.

Seven

By the next day, Rachel had learnt most of her lines. She knew them nearly as well as Nick knew his. The words kept reminding her of Mike, the day before.

Good night, good night! she read. *Parting is such sweet sorrow That I shall say goodnight till it be morrow.*

As Nick read his final lines, Rachel glanced over at Mike. He was staring at her. His head gave a tiny movement, the smallest of shakes, and she knew that they couldn't get away with him giving her a lift home. Her mother was at another governor's meeting tonight. There were a lot of extra ones this term, for some reason. Rachel wanted to see if Mike could come round for an hour. It shouldn't be too dangerous if he parked his car on a side street and came down the back alley. But she couldn't tell him.

When the rehearsal was over, Nick walked home with her part of the way.

"You were good," he told her. "I wasn't sure you would be, but you are."

"Thanks. So were you."

"I wondered ..."

He slowed down. Rachel sensed what he was going to ask and wished that he wouldn't.

"Yes?"

"Whether you're doing anything this weekend. There's a film I really think you'll ..."

"It's not a good idea," Rachel said.

"I meant as friends," Nick said. "We're still friends, aren't we?"

"Of course we are," Rachel said, slowly. "But it's still not a good idea."

"All right," Nick said, sullenly. "See you."

He turned up the hill, leaving Rachel to walk home alone. Rachel felt sorry for Nick, but not for long. As soon as Mum went out, Rachel rang Mike. Mr Hansen answered the phone. Rachel hung up. She wouldn't see her English teacher that night. The frustration was almost too much to bear.

In Friday's lesson, she couldn't take her eyes off him. It was weird, being able to see, but not touch or kiss him. Rachel was worried that Mike would change his mind, decide that seeing her was too dangerous. She tried to linger at the end of class that day, but Ms Howard was there, observing his lesson. After school, Rachel rang his home again, at four-thirty. This time, Mike answered.

"I'm sorry," he told her. "You've got the wrong number."

"I miss you," Rachel said, and hung up.

She decided she was falling in love with him. She'd thought she loved Carl, last summer, but that feeling didn't come close to this one. Rachel felt a new confidence, a new excitement, like she was reaching for a piece of magic: something she'd heard about, but never believed in before.

Rachel was at her father's that weekend. She and Mike would be within walking distance of each other. Maybe they could arrange a date for Saturday night, if they could work out somewhere that they wouldn't be spotted. But Rachel couldn't get through to tell him where she'd be.

On Saturday morning, Rachel took the bus to Dad's. The Shogun wasn't in the drive and Rachel thought for a moment that the family was out. She had a key, but wasn't sure if she could remember the code to the burglar alarm. However, when she rang the doorbell, Dad answered it.

"Where is everybody?" Rachel asked.

"Clarissa's taken the kids to her mum's. She said to tell you she's sorry, but her mother's been ill and ..."

"It's OK," Rachel said, though she would have liked to see the children. It had been weeks.

"Are you going out tonight?" Dad asked.

"I don't think so," Rachel said, hedging her bets. "But I promised to ring someone up. Why, did you have plans for us?"

"Nothing special," Dad said.

They ate lunch together. Her father was a good cook. He made pizza with fresh anchovies and sundried tomatoes. They had a mixed green salad on the side, which Rachel helped prepare. She noticed that the balsamic vinegar in the dressing cost over a fiver. Dad put Hellman's reduced calorie mayonnaise on the table. At home, she and Mum still used salad cream.

"Actually," he said, "I have a favour to ask you."

"Go ahead."

"You know it's Valentine's day on Tuesday?"

"Sure."

"You're not doing anything or seeing anyone at the moment, are you?"

"Not really."

Dad looked gratified. "I wondered if you'd babysit for us, then. You know, Clarissa's been a bit down lately, and I'd like to take her out for a romantic meal, the works."

"Fine," Rachel said, unable to believe her luck. She prayed that Mike was free.

"We won't be back till late. I'll get you a taxi, or drop you off at school in the morning."

"I'll stay the night," Rachel said.

"Great. Usual overnight fee." Dad paid more if she stayed the night.

"Fine."

"One other thing ..." Dad poured Rachel some more Aqua Libra. "I've got to pop out for a couple of hours this afternoon – a colleague with a crisis. Do you mind awfully?"

"No," Rachel insisted. "I have lines to learn, and loads of schoolwork to do. I'll go up to my room."

"You're sure you don't mind?"

"Stay out as long as you like."

The minute he'd gone, Rachel rang Mike. He answered on the second ring.

"It's me. Can you talk?"

"I can," Mike said. "Where are you?"

"I'm at my Dad's," she said. "In Mapperley Park. He's out for at least two hours. Can you come over, now?"

"Try and stop me."

"Hurry," she urged, and gave him the address.

Ten minutes later, he was there. The teacher wore torn jeans and a scruffy sweater. He hadn't shaved. For a moment, they were like awkward strangers.

"I parked the car down the road," he said. "This is a bit of a contrast with your mum's place, isn't it?"

"Dad's upwardly mobile," Rachel told him. "Why don't we go upstairs?"

He followed her. Rachel felt more nervous than she'd ever felt about anything. But he was older. He would know exactly what to do. While waiting, she'd changed into a brown skirt of Clarissa's which unbuttoned down the side. Clarissa would never know. Beneath her cashmere sweater, Rachel wore no bra. She closed the door behind them.

"It was such a rush," Mike said, as they fumbled off each other's clothes. "I didn't bring anything with me. Have you ... are you ... safe?"

"It's fine," Rachel lied.

It wasn't fine. But Rachel didn't know how to talk about sex. Certainly not how to talk about it with a man. Especially an older one. Rachel hadn't planned this. She didn't carry condoms in her purse, like some girls at school. Maybe Mike could go out and buy some. But she'd already lied, said she was safe. It would be so embarrassing to admit it now, and they were both so excited. She didn't want to stop ...

It was all right, Rachel rationalized. This first time, she didn't want anything between them. She began to pull off his jeans. Then they were both naked, embracing. The feel of his body against hers was as exciting as she'd imagined. Rachel was ready for what they were about to do. Even so, Mike found it awkward to get inside her. They kept kissing and whispering endearments to each other, but Mike seemed embarrassed and Rachel didn't know how to help him.

Then they were doing it. Rachel had been expecting it to hurt, and it did, but she was surprised by how quickly it was over, how messy the whole thing was. Afterwards, Mike held her very tightly. He kept whispering, "I can't believe this is happening." Neither could she.

When they'd dressed, they still had some time. Like new acquaintances, they talked about groups they liked and concerts Mike had been to. They discussed films and TV shows and places they wanted to visit. The only thing that they avoided talking about was school. Then they were standing inside the door, getting ready for him to go. Rachel told him about Tuesday night.

"That's wonderful," he said. "What time shall I come?"

"Both kids are usually asleep by half-eight," she said. "Dad and Clarissa won't be back before half-eleven. Why don't you come at nine to be on the safe side? Then we'll have a good two hours."

"Great," Mike told her.

They kissed again.

"God, Rachel," he said. "You're so beautiful. You make me feel so lucky."

"Me too," she said, stroking his face before he left.

When he was gone, Rachel tidied her room, returned Clarissa's skirt, then took some books downstairs to make it look like she was working there. Rachel felt strangely calm. She was a woman now. Mike hadn't told her he loved her, and she hadn't said the words to him. Yet. She didn't want to push her luck, to scare him off. He'd been uneasy, Rachel knew, when he realized that she was a virgin. She didn't want to remind him how young she was.

Suddenly, for no reason that she could think of, Rachel found herself crying. She had a good weep, then cleaned herself up and was happily making notes for a history essay when Dad came in, three and a half hours after he'd left.

"I can't believe you did that," Becky said, as they walked into school together on Monday morning. "Unprotected sex and a one-night stand . . ."

"Afternoon," Rachel corrected.

"What on earth were you thinking of?"

"He was cute," Rachel said.

She'd made up a story about a boy she sort of knew, who lived near her dad, and how he'd come round to her house on Saturday afternoon, while Dad was out.

"Are you seeing him again?" Becky asked.

Rachel shrugged. "I think he has a girlfriend."

"He told you that?"

"There was a photo in his bedroom."

"Wait a minute, I thought you were in *your* bedroom."

"We were," Rachel improvised quickly. "But I've been in his bedroom before. We didn't do anything then."

Becky sighed. "How old is this guy?"

Rachel thought about telling Becky he was Mike's age, but decided she might find that a bit gross. Anyway, Rachel didn't know exactly how old Mike was. For obvious reasons, they hadn't discussed ages.

"Nineteen, twenty ... he's a student, home for the weekend."

"Then he ought to know better," Becky said, sternly. "I'm taking you into town after school today."

"What for?"

"The morning-after pill."

"It's already two mornings after."

"I think it still works. Weren't you listening in those social education lessons last term?"

Rachel had to confess that she wasn't.

"So go on then," Becky said. "Tell me."

"What?"

"Tell me what it was like."

Rachel told her. That was why she'd made it all up, so that

she could share the real experience with her friend. For better or worse, they were equals again.

There was no rehearsal after school that day. During the English lesson, Mike barely looked at her. They would have to be even more careful now. Still, Rachel couldn't take her eyes off him. The class had finished reading the play through, and were going over various scenes in detail.

"Why do Romeo and Juliet fall in love so suddenly?" the teacher asked, then proceeded to answer his own question. "Some people argue that they're destined for each other. A case can also be made for their romance as youthful rebellion: subconsciously, they want to show up their elders and the stupid feud between the two families. Then there's the romantic view: love at first sight."

"What about the lust theory?" Becky suggested. "They fancy each other like crazy and can't wait to start bonking?"

People laughed. Rachel waited, curious to hear Mike's reply to that one, but he only smiled. There was a hint of alarm in his face. He was worried that she might have told her friend their secret.

After school, Rachel and Becky took the bus into town. They often went shopping in the city together on Saturdays, but today was different. Rachel was very nervous, but tried not to let it show. Becky led Rachel to the Safe Sex Centre in Hockley. It was an advice centre. They had posters for it in school. Becky had been going there since Christmas. It was really relaxed, she promised.

A bell rang as the girls went in. Rachel got a fleeting impression of the place. It had pink doors and grey carpets. There were endless leaflets about HIV and AIDS. Posters reminded Rachel why she'd come here. *How do you like your eggs in the morning*? asked one. *Fertilized or unferti-lized*? There were several about condoms. *Condom sense is common sense. 101 uses for a condom.* A black and white poster showed a naked couple embracing. *And she's too embarrassed to ask him to use a condom?* it said. Reading the words made Rachel feel rather foolish.

Less than half a minute passed between the bell ringing and a woman in casual clothes coming out to greet them. Without asking why they were there, she ushered the girls up some stairs and into a private room.

"How can I help?" the nurse asked, when all three of them were sitting down. At first, Rachel was too embarrassed to say anything.

"Is it one of you," the nurse went on, "or do you both need some help?"

"It's her," Becky said. "I'm already registered here."

The woman gave Rachel a sympathetic smile. "Take your time," she said.

"I want the morning-after pill," Rachel said, slowly.

"You've had unprotected sex?"

Rachel nodded.

"When?"

"Saturday afternoon. Is it too late?"

"No," the nurse told her. "You've got up to seventy-two hours for after-sex emergency contraception – that's what we call it. Now then, why don't I take a few details? I don't need your name, but I do need a date of birth."

Rachel worried. When they found out that she was only fifteen, would they refuse to help her? But the date of birth turned out to be for the centre's statistics, not the law. The nurse gave her instructions on taking emergency contra-ception.

"You'll need to come back in six weeks for a check up," she finished. "When you leave, we'll give you a card with a number on it. You should bring it every time you come here. OK?"

Rachel nodded. "Will you give me the pills here?"

"No. You'll have to go to the Teenage Family Planning Clinic for a prescription. But, first, there are a few things I'd like to go over with you."

The nurse gave Becky and Rachel a demonstration about how to use condoms: putting them on, taking them off, not using flavoured ones for penetrative sex, and not flushing used ones down the loo because they didn't degrade.

"I don't want to use condoms," Rachel said. "I want to go on the pill."

"Why?"

"It's more reliable."

"It is if you remember to take it," the nurse told her. "The clinic can sort that out, too, but we don't recommend that you use the pill alone. It's too easy to make mistakes, and catch sexually transmitted diseases. There's no cure for HIV, no sure way for you to tell who's got it. What we recommend is belt and braces: the pill and a condom. That way, you're much less likely to get pregnant. Tell me, are you in a steady relationship?"

Without looking at Becky, Rachel nodded.

"How long have you been together?"

"Two weeks," Rachel said. She could hardly say two days. Two weeks seemed a short time to wait before you started having sex with someone. But the nurse didn't seem surprised. She took Rachel's blood pressure.

"You'll probably be prescribed the combined pill," she said, "but you should be aware that it can take three to six months to get used to it. Some girls get side effects. It can take a little while to find which is the right pill for you."

"Does it work straight away?"

"You need to wait seven days, unless you start taking it on the first day of your period. Then you must take it regularly. If you delay for more than twelve hours at any time, your system's not protected. It wakes up, and you can become pregnant."

On her way out, the nurse gave Rachel a green card, like a credit card, with a number on it. The two girls walked up to the Teenage Clinic.

"That wasn't so bad, was it?" Becky said.

Rachel shook her head. She felt shell-shocked.

The family planning doctor repeated the things the nurse had told her about the morning-after pill. She should take two lots of two, twelve hours apart. Rachel was likely to feel queasy, or worse, and shouldn't make plans to do anything tonight. Tomorrow, she should be sick. The pills could delay her period or bring it on early. It was important that she went back for a check up after six weeks.

Rachel took her pills after dinner that night and felt lousy for the rest of the evening. Mum was out, visiting Tina Scott, but Rachel wasn't tempted to call Mike. She woke up early the next morning, still feeling queasy, and took her other two pills. Then she told her mum that she felt too ill to go to school and went back to bed. Two or three hours later Rachel rushed to the bathroom and was sick. The pills had worked. She didn't need to go back to the doctor for more. Only as she got back into bed did Rachel remember that it was Valentine's day.

Eight

"Are you sure you're well enough to babysit?" Mum asked that evening.

"I'm fine," Rachel insisted, though she wasn't a hundred per cent.

"You're very dressed up for an evening at your father's."

Rachel had on a black, woollen dress which had once been Mum's. She felt sexy in it. "It's what I feel like wearing," she said.

Mum gave her a glance which was almost suspicious. "And you're sure you're over whatever it was?"

"Yes. I must have eaten something which didn't agree with me."

"I'll run you to your father's, to be on the safe side."

It was unusual for Mum to drive Rachel to Dad's. She didn't like driving at the best of times, especially in the dark. Nor did she like going anywhere near Dad's expensive house. From what Rachel knew, their divorce had been very acrimonious. Mum got their tiny terraced house, but never had enough money. She still resented not having finished university and blamed it on Dad. At least, that was what Rachel thought. Mum rarely talked about Dad.

"Is it this one or the next one?"

"This one."

They turned up Tavistock Drive.

"You're sure you've got everything for school tomorrow?

You're not taking another day off if you're out babysitting tonight."

"Yes. I'll be fine. Thanks for the ride."

Dad and Clarissa were waiting to go out.

"They're both in bed. I said you'd go up and read them a story," Clarissa said. "Phoebe's quite upset that she hasn't seen you since Christmas."

"OK," Rachel told her.

Dad wore the new overcoat Clarissa had bought him for Christmas, beneath which Rachel could see a fancy silk tie. Clarissa, as far as Rachel could see, had made less effort. She was wearing, Rachel noted with amusement, the skirt she had borrowed on Saturday afternoon. Dad gave her the number of the restaurant they'd be at.

"I expect you'll be in bed by the time we're back," he said.

I expect I'll be in bed long before then, Rachel thought, seeing them out.

Phoebe and Rowan were happy to see her. They both seemed a little clingy and Rachel had trouble getting away. After twenty minutes, she managed to escape and ring Mike.

It was half-past eight. She'd told him to come at nine, but he might assume that it was off because Rachel had missed school today. There was a coal fire burning in the grate. As his phone rang, Rachel imagined herself making love to Mike on the rug in front of it. They would probably be safer, though, in her bedroom, in case one of the kids came down.

The phone was answered. Rachel prayed it would be Mike, not Phil.

"It's me," she said. "Can you talk?"

"Yes. Phil's taken Tracey out to dinner."

"I'm at Dad's. The kids should be asleep by now. Come round as soon as you can. Tap on the window like we said."

"Great. Are you all right? When you weren't in school today ..."

"It was nothing," Rachel said. "A twenty-four hour thing. I'm over it."

Should she tell Mike what really happened? Rachel didn't think so. She wanted him to think of her as a grown up, not as a young virgin too embarrassed to ask him to take precautions. Tonight, though, Rachel would be more assertive. She had a handbag full of free condoms from the Safe Sex Centre. She would say that she was on the pill, but ask him to wear one anyway. Like the nurse said: *belt and braces*. After the powerful drugs she'd taken, which still left her feeling a bit nauseous, Rachel was probably safe. But she was taking no chances.

Mike put down the phone, barely able to contain his excitement. He bounded upstairs to the bathroom, ran an electric razor over his face and patted on some aftershave. Saturday still seemed like a dream. He'd been reconciled to not seeing Rachel that weekend. One minute he was putting up a shelf in the living room to hold his CD collection, the next he was driving to her father's house. Fifteen minutes after her phone call they were making love. Tonight, he reminded himself, he must talk about contraception. He'd thought Rachel was on the pill, but then he'd found she was a virgin and realized that she might have been lying. The last thing he wanted to do was get a sixteen-year-old girl pregnant. He put some condoms in his pocket along with a tape and a Valentine's day card.

Rachel slipped the door open seconds after he tapped on

the window. She looked at least nineteen, he thought. They went into the living room and kissed.

"What was wrong with you today?" he asked.

"A tummy bug. Did I miss much?"

He shook his head. They exchanged Valentine's cards. Mike gave Rachel a tape of the latest REM album. They embraced fiercely in front of the fire. Mike wanted her there and then, but Rachel pulled away.

"We'd better go upstairs. Sometimes one of the children comes down because they want a drink, or they've had a bad dream."

"All right," Mike said, then added, "Hey, there's something I've been meaning to ask you."

"What?"

"I've got a spare ticket to see Oasis at the Sheffield Arena, end of the Easter holidays. I got one for Emma but ... would you like to go with me?"

"Would I?" Rachel said, a smile spreading across her whole face.

"Can you square it with your mum?"

"I'll think of something," Rachel said, then hugged him. "You're brilliant."

They went upstairs and undressed each other. On Saturday, they'd both been nervous, and awkward. Mike had been worried about hurting her. Tonight, he was very gentle, and careful. When they were ready, Rachel said, "I've got the pill, but ..."

"It's all right," Mike told her. "I'll wear something, until we're both sure it's safe."

This time, when he was inside her, Rachel seemed to relax, and became more passionate. Her innocence and inexperience excited Mike. Again, it was over far too quickly. Mike checked his watch. It was only twenty-past nine.

"We'll have time to do this again," Mike told Rachel, stroking her back.

"Yes, please," she said.

Naked on the narrow bed, they told each other everything: their parents' divorces, what their childhood was like, the things they meant to do with their lives. Rachel wasn't sure if she wanted to go to university, but she was going to become an actress, she knew that. Mike admired her certainty.

At ten, they made love again, but had to stop.

"What's wrong?" Mike asked.

"I've got a pain," she told him. "It's my tummy again. I'll be all right, but ..."

Her voice trailed away.

"What?"

She put a finger to her lips and they both heard it. People coming in.

"Oh, God," Rachel said, pulling away from him.

"I thought you said ..."

"I know. I know!"

Rachel was frantically getting dressed. Mike did the same.

"I thought you were staying the night," he said.

"I was," Rachel told him. "Maybe I still am. It depends how much Dad's had to drink. He might want to drive me home."

Mike suggested a plan. "I could stay in here. You could tell them you'd gone to bed and I could sneak out when they're asleep."

"It wouldn't work," Rachel told him. "You'd set off the burglar alarm."

Mike sighed. From the landing outside, he heard a man's voice hiss, "Rachel?"

"Wait here," Rachel whispered to Mike. "I'll be back."

She switched off the light before opening the door. Mike heard her tell her father, "I was just getting ready for bed."

Mike sat in the dark, sweating. Suppose he was discovered? Rachel's father would recognize him. What then? Violence, probably. Mike would be out of a job, most likely, and would lose Rachel, too. He didn't know which scared him the most.

Suddenly the door burst open and the light flashed on. Mike jumped.

"Only me," Rachel said, throwing his leather jacket on to the bed. "We're lucky. Dad didn't notice this. You'd left it in the lounge."

Mike put it on. "What's happening?"

"I think Dad and Clarissa had a row. They're not talking. He insists he wants to take me home. I think he just wants to get out of the house."

As she talked, Rachel was shoving things into her overnight bag.

"What am I supposed to do?"

"You'll have to sneak out when Dad's driving me home. Clarissa's bound to either stay in the lounge or go to bed. The alarm won't be on till Dad gets back. If I can, I'll leave the front door on the latch so you don't make much noise. All right?"

"It doesn't sound like I have much choice," Mike said.

"I'm sorry about all this," Rachel said, kissing him. "Night."

"Night."

They hadn't arranged to meet again, Mike realized, with a

pang of regret. But he had more immediate problems to face.

Mike heard the front door close. The idea of walking down the stairs and through the hallway didn't appeal to him, but there was little choice. Even if he were able to climb out of the window and jump into the garden without hurting himself, there was a big fence all around it. He might be trapped.

Mike opened the door a little and listened. The landing was dark. The last thing Mike wanted was to bump into Rachel's stepmother as she was coming up to bed. But it was early. She was probably in the lounge, having a drink in front of the fire.

Mike tiptoed across the landing. There was no sound from downstairs. He would have to risk the stairs. What if someone disturbed him? He would pull his jacket over his face and run out, pretending to be a burglar. It might work.

Mike was halfway down the stairs when the lounge door opened. He ducked, hoping he couldn't be seen from the hall. If she came upstairs now, he was done for. Footsteps crossed the hall. Mike stopped breathing for a few seconds. Then he heard the sound of a phone being dialled.

"Hi, Mum. It's me."

"An unmitigated disaster," Clarissa said, in reply to something. "He said he would, but he won't."

Mike didn't listen closely to the call. He looked at his watch. At this time of night, Stonywood was a five or, at most, a ten-minute drive. Unless Mr Webster stopped off somewhere, he would be back in five minutes.

Clarissa Webster seemed to realize this too. He heard her winding up the call. "Look, I'd better go to bed. I don't want to be up when he comes back. No, I'll sleep in Rachel's room tonight. I made up a fresh bed for her." Mike began to panic. What state had they left the room in? He crept up the stairs, as quietly as he could, while Clarissa was still talking, and straightened the sheets. Then he went back out on to the landing.

She'd hung up. Where could Mike hide? The house had four bedrooms. Clarissa was bound to go into her own bedroom and into Rachel's room and the bathroom. She'd probably check the kids before getting into bed, too. Nowhere was safe.

Mike crept back down the stairs. Rachel's father would be home any moment. He could hear Clarissa moving about in the kitchen. The microwave pinged. She was probably making herself a hot drink to take to bed. As he got to the bottom of the stairs, Mike saw that the kitchen door was open. He saw Clarissa's back, then her profile. She was a slender, pretty woman the right side of thirty. For a moment, he thought that she was going to turn and see him. Instead, she turned the other way, reached over to pick up something, and was out of sight.

Mike dashed across the hall, into the porch. If Rachel's father came back this minute, he would bump into him. Rachel had left the door on the latch, as she'd promised. Gently, Mike tugged it open, then let the latch go. He pushed the door closed behind him as quietly as he could. Then he ran up the path and out on to the street. He got into his car just as a black Shogun swept past him and turned into the Webster's drive.

Never again, he told himself, as he drove home. *This has to stop*.

Nine

"Good night, good night! Parting is such sweet sorrow
That I shall say goodnight till it be morrow."

Rachel made her exit, then waited while Nick did the scene's final lines with his usual studied casualness. They joined Ms Howard in the corner of the drama room, where she went through several points about their performances. The half-term holiday started tomorrow. There would be no more rehearsals for ten days.

"Anything to add, Mr Steadman?" Ms Howard asked when she was done.

"I don't think so," Mike said. "It's coming along well."

"Walk you home?" Nick offered as the two teachers conferred.

Rachel glanced hopefully over at Mike, but it was clear he wouldn't get away. "Thanks," she said, absentmindedly.

The streets of Stonywood were safe, compared to parts of the inner city, but Rachel still felt uneasy walking home alone when it was turning dark. A girl from school had been pulled into an alley and raped the year before. At the time, Mum made Rachel carry an alarm in her handbag, though she'd since lost it.

"You seem different somehow," Nick said, as they left the school site. "More confident."

"Maybe it's the hair," Rachel said, then regretted her flippancy. Nick knew her well enough to know that she'd changed. But she couldn't tell him why.

"Have you got a new boyfriend?" Nick asked, zeroing in on the truth.

Rachel shook her head. "No boys until after the exams," she lied. "The play's a big enough distraction."

"You could see me," Nick suggested, gently. "You've got to see me anyway."

Rachel was silent. When would he give up?

"You never really explained why you finished with me," Nick added.

"I did," Rachel insisted, though, now she thought about it, she couldn't remember what reasons she'd given him, couldn't quite recall what reasons she'd given herself, except that he wasn't old enough. Nick didn't press the point.

"It must be the play that's changed you," Nick said. "You really can act. I'm impressed. I guess that's what's making you more ..." He didn't finish the sentence, but he didn't have to. When Rachel looked at him, desire was written all across his face.

"I nearly sent you a Valentine," Nick said, as they got to the end of her street. "But I didn't know if ..."

Rachel stopped and kissed him on the cheek. "I'm glad you didn't," she said. "Let's enjoy acting together. OK?"

He gave her his sad-eyed smile. "OK. See you after half-term."

He turned back and, with the smallest of waves, walked away.

Mum wasn't back from work. Rachel put her REM tape on the stereo downstairs, cranking up the volume until it made the shelves shake. Heavy metal chords ran through her body as she threw herself around the living room. All the songs seemed to be about sex. Her favourite was called "Crush with Eyeliner". The singer said he was smitten, infatuated. It was the way Rachel felt about Mike.

That night, Mum had to go out for some kind of extra school governors' meeting. Rachel rang Mike, but Phil Hansen answered the phone. She wished her lover lived alone. There was nothing to do but spend the evening watching TV. BBC1 had a new series about moral dilemmas, *Do the Right Thing*: tonight, should teachers be allowed to have love affairs with their pupils? It looked really tacky, but Rachel couldn't stop herself watching. At the beginning, the studio audience voted a unanimous "no" to the question. By the end, however, after a silly dramatization which ended with the teacher being sacked, two thirds of the audience had changed their minds, because the couple were *in love*.

"What's this rubbish?" Mum asked, as she walked back into the house.

Rachel told her.

"I don't know what the BBC's coming to," Mum commented, tartly.

"It's a serious issue, though," Rachel said. "You know, should they be allowed to ..."

"Oh, it's a serious issue all right," Mum said, "but I don't want to talk about it now. I want a bath."

Rachel left the subject, though she didn't want to. Discussing the programme would have been interesting. Rachel might have been able to work out how Mum would react to her being with Mike. But Mum was on her way upstairs.

"How was your meeting?" Rachel called to her.

"Depressing. I'll tell you about it later."

"Tracey not coming over tonight?" Mike asked Phil, as he finished his fish and abandoned the last few chips.

"Nah. Girls' night out. Fancy going to the Dover Castle later on, playing some pinball?"

"Fine by me."

The phone rang in the other room. Mike found himself hurrying to answer it. The voice on the other end wasn't Rachel's. It was his mother.

They had a desultory conversation. Yes, the job was going fine. No, he hadn't heard from Emma, didn't expect to. Yes, he remembered that it was his father's birthday next week, though why Mum was reminding Mike when she'd divorced Dad three years ago was beyond him. Finally, he was sorry, but he was too busy to visit her over half-term.

"Got plans for half-term?" Phil asked, when he returned to the dining room.

Mike shook his head. "I want to get my lessons properly sorted for next half-term. The play's going to take up so much time that if I don't do it now, I never will. Anyway, I'm still totally skint. Are you and Tracey going somewhere?"

Phil shook his head. Mike didn't know whether or not to be relieved. If Phil went away for a day or two, Mike could have Rachel over. But maybe it would be best for them not to have the opportunity. If things went any further with Rachel, Mike could see himself falling into a hole which he could never crawl out of. He was crazy about Rachel, but the whole thing was too risky. He ought to let her down gently. Yet... The phone rang once more. This time, Phil answered it.

"Dead again. You reckon some kid at school's got our number and started playing silly beggars?"

"It's possible," Mike said. "Maybe you should go ex-directory."

"Too late for that," Phil said. "Ready for the pub?"

"Give me five minutes," Mike said.

He went upstairs for a wash, thinking about Rachel. That was bound to have been her, for the second time today. She'd probably snuck out of the house to a phone box to call him. How could he give her up? Just the thought of being with her excited him, even if it had to be in the back seat of his car. He found himself getting angry with Phil. *Why wouldn't he go away?* Next week, during the day, Mike would be able to phone Rachel at home while her mother was at work. But it was too risky to go to her house, no matter how much he wanted to.

Mike went into his room to get some money. He didn't get paid for a week and he was short. He rifled through three pairs of jeans. Sometimes he stuffed a note into a back pocket. Nothing there. He reached into the breast pocket of the smarter of his two school jackets and pulled out some junk. Unravelling a tissue, he was relieved to find a fiver. There was something else there, too. He turned it over: a beermat. Written on the back of it was Sarah Poole's phone number.

Sarah would probably be free over half-term. She was nice. He ought to call her. But he knew he wouldn't. It was pointless. There was no way that Mike could form a relationship with anyone else while his mind was full of Rachel. And there was no way that he should call Rachel, either.

But he knew that he would.

Ten

On the second Sunday afternoon of half-term, Rachel tried to get down to the homework she'd been putting off for the whole holiday. There'd been days when she tried, but couldn't get anything done, not even a *Romeo and Juliet* essay for Mike. "Write extracts from Juliet's diary for the first two acts of the play" was the assignment. *Met this great guy at a party*, Rachel wrote. *I was walking on air until Nursey told me the bad news – he's a Montague!*

It didn't work. Rachel was trying to write like a naive teenager, but she didn't feel like a teenager any more. She was a woman, and all she wanted was to spend time with Mike. But it wasn't easy. Rachel had had no babysitting jobs over half-term and Phil Hansen didn't go away. She and Mike had only managed two meetings: an hour in the maths teacher's rather shabby house on Monday, when Phil was shopping, and a hurried coupling in the back of Mike's car in an empty car park at night, when Rachel was supposed to be at Becky's.

Rachel wished she could see Mike when she wanted, that they could go dancing together, kiss in public, walk the streets hand in hand. Why shouldn't they? Rachel had thought about it long and hard: as far as she was concerned, they were doing nothing wrong. The age difference between her and Mike was less than that between Dad and Clarissa. They had more in common than most couples she knew.

What they were doing was against the law, true. So were lots of things which shouldn't be, things which didn't hurt anybody.

But Rachel did see advantages in the way things were. There was something very exciting about secrecy, about snatched meetings and hurried sex. It was like living your life in a movie which hurtled from scene to scene. Rachel's life was a series of fast-forward flickering images, cutting from one scene with Mike Steadman to the next. The bits in between didn't count for anything.

Tomorrow she would be back at school, where she would see Mike every day. In some ways, that was worse. She hated seeing Mike and not being able to touch him. She wanted to talk to him as a lover, not a pupil.

Mum was in the kitchen, cooking. The radio was on. Mum wouldn't be able to hear the phone. Rachel went down to the hall and dialled Mike's number. He'd said that Phil would be seeing Tracey today – either this afternoon or evening. Rachel needed to see him. It didn't matter where or how. He answered the phone with his usual brusque "Hello".

"Mike, it's me. Can you talk?"

There was a deathly pause. "Er, this isn't Mike, it's Phil. Who is this?"

Rachel choked. Mr Hansen's voice was deeper than usual. Maybe he had a cold. Rachel nearly put down the phone, but that would drop Mike in it. Instead, she changed her voice slightly.

"It's Cynthia," she said, picking the first name which came to mind. "Is Mike there?"

"He's in the bath," Phil told her. "Can I get him to call you back?"

"It's all right," Rachel replied, slowly affecting a more upper-class voice. "I'll catch him later."

She hung up, then slammed her fist several times against the telephone table.

"Who's Cynthia?"

"Pardon?"

Mike had just got out of the bath and was preparing some lessons at the kitchen table. Phil was having dinner with Tracey's parents that evening, and Mike was hoping Rachel would call, that he'd be able to pick her up and bring her over.

"A girl called Cynthia rang you up, wouldn't leave a message."

Mike considered lying, but he'd never been any good at it. "I don't know any Cynthias," he said.

"Me neither," Phil told him. "At first, she thought I was you. When she found out I wasn't, her voice seemed to change. Maybe it was a kid from school, messing around."

"Maybe," Mike said.

"Although," Phil went on, "I didn't know that any of the kids at school knew we shared a house."

"I haven't told anyone," Mike assured him, "but you know how schools are: the most insignificant bits of gossip spread like wildfire."

Rachel didn't ring. Mike considered calling her at home, hanging up if her mother answered. He decided against it. Too risky. When he'd finished working, he played some CDs and read the Sunday papers. He microwaved a Chinese meal from Marks & Spencer's and drank some red wine with it, the wine he'd bought to share with Rachel. Then he turned on the TV and dozed off.

He was woken by the phone. Mike snapped awake, thinking for a moment that he was late for school. It was ten to eight, he saw. Had he been here all night? Then he realized that it was still evening. He turned off the TV and picked up the phone. It was silent.

"Rachel?" Mike said, softly. "It's OK. Phil's gone out."

"I'm sorry about that," Rachel told him. "It was just ... he sounded like you and I was so desperate to hear your voice, to see you ... It's been days."

"I'm here now," Mike said, warmly. "Can I come and collect you?"

"I'm in a phone box," Rachel told him. "I told Mum I needed to borrow a maths book from Carmen. She won't expect me to be away long."

"You can call her from here," Mike said. "Say you've decided to stay and do some work with Carmen. You can even borrow one of Phil's textbooks if you want to make it look convincing."

"All right," Rachel said. She told him where she was.

Mike got in the car and sped over there. On a quiet night like this, he could reach Stonywood in eight minutes. Mike's heart leapt. What pleasure was there which compared with getting something just after you'd given up on it? But it was more than that, Mike realized. He would have to stop fooling himself. All week, he hadn't been able to get Rachel off his mind. He felt about her in a way he'd never felt for anyone before. Not even Emma.

It was drizzling. Rachel waited in a phone box on the main road, stepping out as Mike's car pulled up. Ten minutes later, he was pouring her a glass of wine in his bedroom.

"I've missed you so much," Rachel said.

"Me, too," Mike whispered. "I love you."

Rachel pulled him to her. This was the first time that either of them had said the words.

"I love you, too," she told him.

Mike felt something inside himself filling up.

Afterwards, as they lay together in each other's arms, they talked about the future.

"When I've finished school," Rachel said, "we'll be able to see each other openly, won't we?"

"I don't see why not," Mike said, "as long as we don't rub it in people's faces."

The future seemed a long way off. He'd spent most of the week trying to think of ways to finish with her, failing.

"Will you get your own place?" Rachel asked.

"Who knows?" Mike said. "Maybe we can get a place together."

Rachel gave him a long, lingering kiss, leaving him in no doubt how she felt about that idea. "I might need to move out of home," she said, with anxiety in her voice, "if Mum doesn't approve of me going out with you. Mum can get ... Oh, God!" There was blind panic in her eyes.

"What?" Mike asked.

"I forgot to ring Mum up! She'll be worried sick."

Naked, Rachel ran downstairs to use the phone. Two minutes later she was back, looking chastened.

"She'd rung Carmen half an hour ago. She knew I wasn't there."

Mike swore. "What did you tell her?"

"Nothing. I said I'd explain when I got home. I'd better go straight away."

They dressed hurriedly. Mike didn't know how to deal with this. One minute they were talking about moving in together, the next he was having to rush Rachel back to her mother's. It made him feel like a guilty teenager himself.

Mike got on to the ringroad and sped towards Stonywood. Rain poured down.

"What will you tell her?" he asked.

"I don't know," Rachel said. "She'll guess I've been seeing a boy – or doing drugs. She worries about that, too."

"Is there anyone you can say you've been with?"

Mike expected her to say Nick, but, instead, Rachel mentioned a boy called Carl.

"Mum doesn't know where he lives, so she couldn't check him out. But ..."

Suddenly, Mike was aware of a flashing light behind them. He swore repeatedly.

"Not now," Rachel said. "What will you tell them?"

"There's nothing *to* tell them," Mike said. "I was speeding, that's all."

"How old shall I say I am?" Rachel asked, as Mike pulled off the road. "Seventeen, eighteen?"

"They're not going to ask," Mike assured her. "I just hope I'm under the limit." He got out of the car.

"In a hurry, sir?" the policeman asked.

"I'm sorry," Mike said. "I know I was breaking the speed limit."

The policeman nodded. "Had you noticed, sir, that it's raining, and there's a lot of water on the road?"

"Yes."

"Would you say that those were circumstances in which it was appropriate to drive faster than the speed limit?"

Mike felt like he was dealing with a particularly pedantic teacher, but he had to humour him, to get it over with as quickly as possible.

"No," he said.

"Have you been drinking at all, sir?"

"I had a little red wine, but it was a while ago now."

Actually, not expecting to drive, he'd had nearly half a bottle. He might be under the limit, but it would be a close thing.

"Blow into this, please. Harder. That's it. Keep going."

From the car, Rachel watched with undisguised concern as the policeman examined the breathalyzer. Mike wondered why she was worried about her age.

"You're in the clear, sir. Just. I should warn you ..."

Mike kept nodding as he got the lecture on drinking and driving, then agreed to take his papers into Radford Road police station within the next few days. By the time he got back into the car they'd been stopped for nearly fifteen minutes. He told Rachel what had happened.

"I don't know what I'm going to tell Mum," she said.

They left the ringroad and Mike drove into Stonywood at twenty-eight miles per hour. As they neared Rachel's street, he asked, "Why were you worried about your age, Rachel? You're sixteen, aren't you?"

She was silent. He stopped the car and turned to her. Rachel shook her head. "Not until April."

Mike groaned. "You look so old. I assumed ..."

Rachel began to cry. Her voice was that of a sulky teenager. "Why does it matter how old I am? I thought you loved me ..."

He pulled her to him, trying to take it all in. "I do love you, I do. It's just that what we're doing is against the law. We'll have to be even more careful now."

"You're not going to finish with me?" Rachel said, through her tears.

"I couldn't if I tried," Mike told her.

Rachel ran through the rain back to her house. Mike didn't start the car. He was lost in thought. She'd let him think she was sixteen, he knew that. In Rachel's position, he'd probably have done the same thing. But she was jail bait. And her birthday wasn't until after Easter, mere weeks before she went on study leave. If word got round that they'd moved in together – even that they were going out with each other – people were bound to guess that it had been going on since before Easter. They would guess that it happened during the play.

But Mike couldn't give her up. It didn't matter how old she was. If Rachel wasn't a woman yet, she was on the cusp of becoming one – the sort of woman who men would knock down doors to get to. Only he'd got there first.

There was only one thing for it. They would keep the relationship quiet until the end of the school year. Then his contract would be up and he'd get another job. At a new school. No one would have to know that his girlfriend had been in his year-eleven class the year before. That was it. Keep a lid on things for five months and they'd be home and dry. He started the engine.

"And where have you been?"

When telling lies, Rachel had read somewhere, it was best to stay as close to the truth as possible. That way, you were much less likely to be caught.

"With a boy."

"Who?" Mum said, sharply.

"No one you know."

Rachel looked at the ground. She hated this kind of confrontation.

"And what were you doing? How come it took you so long to get home?"

"We were in his car," Rachel said. "After I rang you, he was rushing me home. I'd have been here half an hour ago, only he got stopped for speeding."

Mum shook her head. "That's not the whole story. Have you been taking something?"

"No!"

Mum came closer to her. "Can I smell your breath?"

"What is this," Rachel complained, "the Gestapo?"

Mum leant forward. "You've been drinking."

"I had a glass of wine."

"And was he drinking too?"

"They breathalyzed him. He was clear."

Mum tried to put her arms around her daughter, but Rachel shook her away.

"I thought we could talk to each other about things. Who is this boy? Where did you meet him?"

"It doesn't matter."

"How old is he? Tell me that at least."

"Eighteen," Rachel lied.

"Are you having sex with him?"

Mum was crying, Rachel saw. She was hurting her. But she'd already gone deeper than she'd ever meant to go. All she'd wanted to tell Mum tonight was that she was round at Carmen's, doing maths. Why did she have to tell her more than that?

"I'm on the pill," she said. "I'll have sex when I want to. But it's private. I don't ask you about things like that."

"I'd tell you if you asked me," Mum said, softly.

"I know what I'm doing," Rachel insisted.

"I hope so," Mum said. "I really hope so."

Eleven

Every Monday before school started there was a staff briefing. The first Monday after half-term, the only spare seats were in a group which included Sarah Poole. Seeing Mike sit down, Sarah turned away. She'd expected him to call her, Mike realized, and felt snubbed.

The group were talking about what they'd done over half-term. Paul Kelly, who taught French, had been to Paris, where it had rained. Most people had stayed home. A lot of DIY had been done.

"Did anyone see that Terry Wogan thing that was on the Friday we broke up?" Jan from PE asked. "Now that was really silly."

"Why did you keep watching then?" Paul Kelly asked.

"Well, the boy who was supposed to be having an affair with his teacher was rather gorgeous."

"That's the trouble," Paul Kelly said. "An eighteen-year-old boy dating an older woman is an acceptable fantasy. The hypocrisy comes when male teachers are condemned for dating teenage girls."

"You'd know all about that, would you?" Sarah Poole interjected, getting a laugh. "Seriously," she added, "everyone knows that it's wrong for a teacher of any age to use his position to sleep with his – or her – students."

"But what if they fall in love?" Jan asked. "It happens all the time – bosses and secretaries, university lecturers and students ... You can make rules against it, but you can't stop it going on. I knew this girl who ..."

"You can if the rules are backed up by strong sanctions," Sarah interrupted. "People are always going on about love matches – pupil/teacher marriages that have lasted. But they're the exception, not the rule. Those relationships are unequal in a lot of ways: power, money and experience. They're wrong."

Jan made a second attempt to start telling an anecdote, but Sarah kept going. "And think about it: what kind of man enjoys going out with an inexperienced girl years and years younger than him? I'll tell you what sort – the sort of man whose main interest is sex. The sort who's a show-off and too immature to relate to women his own age. And I'll tell you what's worse – nine times out of ten, he gets away with it and the girl has her life ruined."

Sarah was known for getting on her hobby horse and riding the thing for all it was worth. Today, though, she was being taken seriously. Several people started talking at once. Phil looked uncomfortable, even though Mike was the only person there who knew that he was going out with an eighteen-year-old.

"If I could have your attention, ladies and gentlemen," Mrs Perry commanded, and the conversation fell away. Sarah pulled out her Union diary and a pen. Something important must be coming up, if she was going to make notes. Mike, though, was so busy thinking about the conversation he'd just heard that, at first, he didn't take in what Mrs Perry was saying.

"As you're probably aware," the Headteacher began, "this school, like all others, has to make big budget cuts in the next financial year. We're short over a hundred thousand pounds. On the raw figures, we would have to lose at least seven full-time staff."

There was a collective gasp before the Headteacher went on.

"The governors have been meeting over half-term to see how we can make up the gap. They've decided that every department will have to cope with bigger class sizes, fewer free periods and less money to spend on books and equipment." There was a kind of rumbling noise as the Head continued. "But that still leaves us with a large shortfall."

She paused. A deadly hush fell on the staffroom. Sarah scribbled frantically. Mrs Perry gave some financial figures, then spelt out the consequences. "We need to lose the equivalent of at least four full-time teachers. Inevitably, part-time staff will have their hours reduced and some contracts will not be renewed. There will also have to be redundancies."

A kind of muttering broke out. Sarah Poole raised her hand but Mrs Perry ignored her.

"The governors are very anxious to avoid compulsory redundancies if at all possible. Today, I am issuing voluntary redundancy notices. Any teacher over the age of fifty taking early retirement will get full pension enhancement with index-linking from the age of fifty-five."

Mike looked around. There were few teachers over the age of forty, never mind fifty. This was a young staff. More people started talking.

"My door will be open ..." Mrs Perry went on, but she was shouted down by Sarah Poole.

"Can you tell us at what stage compulsory redundancies will be decided?"

"The process has to be completed by May 31st," the Head said, tersely.

"And can you explain why the staff haven't been consulted before now, as they have been in other schools?"

"You *are* being consulted," the Head said. "This week, departments are being asked to consider economies ..."

The bell went for morning school.

"That's not what I meant," Sarah said, then raised her voice still higher. "Emergency Union meeting at twelve-thirty in the drama studio. Please everyone, try and be there."

Although school was meant to be starting, no one left in a hurry. Judith Howard charged over to Sarah. She had a fight scene rehearsal in the drama room that lunch hour, Mike knew. Tough. Mike would go to the meeting, even though what was happening made little difference to him. His temporary contract was no longer likely to be renewed, but so what? He'd already made up his mind to leave.

Not having a tutor group, Mike waited in the staffroom until lessons started. He watched Sarah put up a notice about the meeting.

"Well said," he told her.

She thanked him. "If you want to talk to me about your position ..." she offered.

"Maybe later. Did you have a good half-term?"

"So-so. You?"

Mike shrugged, as if to imply that it hadn't been all that interesting. "I've been meaning to call you," he lied. "Arrange a drink."

"Do that," Sarah said. "But I've got a feeling the next few weeks are going to be very busy. There's bound to be a strike ballot."

Sarah started putting leaflets out on the staffroom tables. Mike had never been keen on politics, not even Union politics. He'd seen the way some people looked at Sarah when she was shouting at the Head – they wrote her off as a neurotic lefty. Mike didn't share all her views, but, at the same time, he admired people who had worked out a position and were prepared to argue it.

Sarah, he thought, had some of the earnest idealism which Mike loved in Rachel. But Sarah's kind of idealism insisted on polarizing arguments, like when she'd been talking about teacher/pupil relationships. Things weren't as black and white as Sarah said, not with him and Rachel. Sarah made everything sleazy, corrupt. It didn't feel that way at all.

In his year-eleven lesson that day, Mike collected in a bunch of assignments. Eight of the kids hadn't finished theirs, and he kept them in over break for a lecture on the importance of keeping deadlines. Rachel, to his surprise, was one of the tardy ones. She didn't meet his eye once during the telling off.

The rehearsals were up to three or four nights a week now, with frequent lunch-hour sessions too. Rachel had to attend about half of them. Mike found that Judith Howard did most of the big scenes as the play got nearer. Mike was rarely on his own with Nick and Rachel. He was reduced, instead, to doing a lot of running around. His head of department had a well worked-out technique, Mike realized, for making you feel involved, then turning you into her dogsbody.

Towards the end of that week, Mike had his regular mentor meeting with Judith. She had observed two of his lessons now. The first was a bit messy, the second a success. He was confident about the third, final one. However, when he suggested getting it over with soon, Judith dismissed the idea.

"It's only a formality, but we'd better leave it until next term, when the play's over and you're bound to have flowered even more."

Mike smiled gracefully, accepting the compliment.

Judith went on, "But I did want to talk to you about this redundancies business."

Mike pretended interest. He mustn't let her know he didn't intend to stay.

"Now I know you'll be feeling at risk," Judith told him, "but I don't want you to worry. We can't afford to lose an English teacher. And if the Head tries to get me to replace you with staff from other subjects who aren't qualified to teach English, I won't have it. So don't start looking for another job just yet."

"I won't," Mike said.

As he drove home, it occurred to him that next term he would be competing with a fresh crop of new teachers, who would be even cheaper to employ than he was. Despite what he'd told Judith, he needed to start applying for jobs soon.

"You look tense," Rachel said, when she came round that night. She was meant to be at Becky's. Mike told her about the Union meeting, the redundancies.

"You'd better not spread it round at school," he added.

"What do you take me for?" Rachel replied, with a withering look. "I knew something was going on, anyway. My mum's a governor, remember? She's been having a lot of extra meetings recently. Is your job in danger?"

"Yes," Mike told her. "But I don't want to stay at Stonywood. I'd like to go somewhere better, with a sixth form."

"Like older girls, do you?" Rachel teased him.

Mike gave her a playful punch. "Also," he said, "when you've left, we need to be able to see each other, without it being secret. That might be difficult if I stay at Stonywood."

Rachel hugged him. It was the first time he'd made this commitment. She seemed to want it, too.

"But I might have trouble getting another job," Mike added.

"No, you won't. You're a great teacher. And if you can't get a job in Nottingham, I'll follow you anywhere. Try and stop me."

Rachel's eyes began to water. Mike held her close, feeling equally emotional. He wiped the tears from her eyes and kissed her. Then Rachel looked at her watch. "You're going to have to take me home. After what happened on Sunday, Mum's given me a midweek curfew. I'm to be home by ten."

Mike drove her back. He'd arranged to meet Phil and Tracey for a drink around ten, and give Phil a lift home. Only after he'd dropped Rachel off did Mike realize that this was the first time they'd met indoors and not gone to bed. All they'd done was enjoy each other's company. Didn't that prove Sarah Poole wrong?

"Get lots of work done?" Phil asked, when Mike walked into the Grosvenor.

"So-so."

Mike remembered that Rachel was supposed to have done her *Romeo and Juliet* essay tonight. It would be interesting to see what excuse she came up with tomorrow.

"We've got some news for you," Tracey told him.

"Yeah?"

For a moment, Mike thought that they were going to get married. But it wasn't quite as dramatic as that.

"Trace and I are going on holiday together over Easter," Phil told him. "Ten days in Corfu."

Mike's eyes lit up. He would have the house to himself.

"After that," Phil went on, "if we can stand each other's company day and night for that long, we're going to move in together."

Mike forced a smile. "Congratulations," he said.

Tracey looked concerned. "Don't worry," she told him. "We won't be kicking you out of your home."

"Tracey's flatmate's got a new job starting in April," Phil explained. "We figured I'd move in with her for a while and, if things work out, I'll put the house on the market and we'll look for somewhere bigger."

"I can find somewhere else," Mike offered. "It seems silly, moving to a rented flat when you own a house."

Phil shook his head. "Trace doesn't want to live in Radford: too rough." He took a swig of beer, then added, in a more sober voice. "I might have to sell the house anyway, after the news this week. The maths department's over-staffed."

Every conversation that day seemed to come back to redundancies. Mike watched as Tracey squeezed Phil's hand. There was no doubting how much they cared for each other. Would Sarah Poole say that they shouldn't be together? Mike wished that he could have Rachel here, too, talking with them, that he could go on holiday with his girlfriend. But maybe, in a few months, he could.

Twelve

"Not seeing your friend tonight?" Mum asked, caustically, over dinner.

Rachel shook her head. "Got an English essay to do. Overdue."

"I thought being in this play was meant to be helping you with your English?"

"It is ... only, it's a silly assignment, that's all."

"You're going off Mr Steadman, are you? He seemed to think highly of you at parents' evening."

Rachel pushed the remains of her food aside without answering the question. "I've had enough," she said. "I'd better do some work."

Since the episode when she'd lied to Mum about going to Carmen's, things had been awkward between them. In the past, when Rachel rowed with Mum, they'd resolved things within a day or two. A late night heart-to-heart would bring them closer together. But this was different. Rachel couldn't tell Mum the truth about what was going on and she didn't want to lie to her. Therefore, whenever Mum tried to get through to Rachel, it only made matters worse.

Rachel was looking forward to staying at her father's that weekend. He and Mum never talked, so Dad didn't know what was going on. He wouldn't quiz her about who she was or wasn't seeing. At nine, Rachel slipped out of the house to call Mike. It was a waste of time. Phil Hansen picked up the phone. Rachel considered calling herself Cynthia again, but Mike had warned her not to. She hung up. Returning home, she opened the front door quietly.

"Rachel, is that you?" Mum called out. She didn't ask where Rachel had been. "Your father phoned and I couldn't find you. He has to cancel this weekend."

Rachel groaned. "Why?"

"He didn't say. Call him back if you like."

"What's the point?" Rachel said, and went up to her room. Now she was sure that Clarissa was having an affair. Maybe her stepmother was even on the verge of leaving Dad. Rachel wished that Dad would open up to her about it.

That weekend, she didn't see Mike. Rachel bought herself an LP by Elastica, who she'd seen on *Top of the Pops*. When the play was over, she wanted to get her hair cut short like the singer, Justine. Rachel's hair was pretty long now, and it irritated her. Rachel taped the LP for Mike, along with the free flexidisc which came with it. Hopefully, he would be impressed. Maybe he would offer to take her to see the group when they played Rock City at the end of the month.

But Rachel didn't get an opportunity to give Mike the tape. The most contact she had with him over the next few days was when he returned her essay with a C-.

Meanwhile, rehearsals staggered on. Rachel felt like she'd hit a plateau. For a few weeks, she'd felt like she was improving in leaps and bounds, but she was no longer getting better. She had to put up with endless, boring fittings for her costumes: long, ridiculous things borrowed from the Lace Market theatre. They succeeded in making her feel like a thirteen-year-old virgin.

"You seem a bit down," Nick told Rachel when they were

walking home together after Thursday's rehearsal. "What is it?"

"I don't know," Rachel said. "Nothing, really."

"Any time you want to talk, about anything," Nick said. "You can with me. You know that."

"I know," Rachel said, and touched his hand, gratefully.

"If you wanted to come round . . ."

Rachel shook her head. "Please, Nick. Don't try so hard."

She'd meant it kindly, but Nick looked hurt. "I've given up trying in the way you mean. You're out of my league. I know that. I still want to be your friend."

"I think that's supposed to be my line," Rachel said, half-heartedly.

Nick turned off with his usual half wave, leaving Rachel feeling vaguely guilty. The nights were lighter now. There was no need for Nick to walk her all the way home, no excuse for Mike to give her a lift. She missed him. It was hard to concentrate on anything when it was days since she'd seen Mike properly.

Rachel felt lonely. Recently, she'd seen little of Becky, and even less of Carmen. Both were working hard in the lead up to the exams. Neither could understand why Rachel cared so little about her studies. The only person who Rachel could really talk with was Mike. But their conversations were snatched things which, most of the time, took second place to sex. Rachel had to see Mike soon, if only for a walk in the park. She had to find a way to meet him.

There was no rehearsal after school on Friday. Rachel resolved to catch Mike at the end of the day. She made an excuse to get out of maths early. Mike had year seven last lesson of the day. The youngsters were always let out of last lesson a couple of minutes early. This was to avoid their being caught in the mad crush of big kids leaving the site and pushing their way on to buses.

The class was still in when Rachel got there. She didn't want to be seen hanging around, so went to the girls' toilets and adjusted her face. Then, hearing footsteps in the corridor, she slipped out again. Rachel slid into Mike's classroom just as the last kid was leaving.

Mike sat behind his desk, head propped up by a fist, looking exhausted. He hadn't noticed her come in. Rachel quickly pulled one of the curtains to so they couldn't be seen from outside. Mike looked up.

"I missed you," she said. "I couldn't stay away."

"But we agreed . . ."

"Please, Mike, just tell me when we can meet."

"Aren't you at your father's?"

"He cancelled again."

Mike thought. "All right. Tomorrow. I'll pick you up in the park at two. If Phil's out we'll go back to the house. If not . . ."

He gave a tired shrug. Rachel wanted to hold, to cuddle him. Mike got up. All around them was the sound of chairs being put up, of children leaving the building. Rachel gave him the tape she'd made for him. Mike thanked her absentmindedly and put it in his bag. Rachel mentioned the concert that was coming up.

"I don't know if I could get out, but . . ."

"That reminds me," Mike interrupted, "I have some good news.

"What?"

"Phil and Tracey are going away for ten days at Easter. I'll have the house to myself."

Rachel could barely contain her excitement, but there was more.

"And they're talking about him moving into her flat when they come back."

"Brilliant!"

Rachel hugged Mike. She found herself kissing him, and being kissed back. Neither of them heard the door open.

"Excuse me, sir."

The couple broke apart as though someone had fired a gun. A small boy was walking into the room. One glance at his disturbed face showed that he had seen what they were doing. Somehow, Mike managed to put on a teacher's voice.

"What is it, Paul?"

"I think I left my pencil case behind."

"Let's look for it, shall we?"

The boy started to back away sheepishly. "I didn't mean to disturb you," he said.

Rachel could feel her face turning a million shades of red.

"No, it's all right, really," Mike said. "Rachel was just going. She ... er ... got a little over enthusiastic in thanking me for some help."

Rachel picked up her bag and hurried out of the room as Mike continued talking. "You won't mention what you saw to anyone, will you? You can see how embarrassing it is for the girl. Now, what colour is that pencil case?"

When Paul Wilks was gone, pencil case in hand, Mike found himself shaking. The boy might only be eleven or twelve and no great shakes in the intellect department, but he knew what was going on, all right. What the hell was Rachel doing, coming into his classroom at the end of school like that? They'd agreed on absolute discretion at school. She'd done the precise opposite.

"Are we going home or what?"

Phil Hansen had walked in, making Mike jump again.

"I've been waiting in the staffroom for ... are you all right? You look like you've seen a ghost."

"I'm fine. It's been a long week, that's all."

Phil frowned, unconvinced.

The two men hardly spoke again until they went for their regular drink in the Dover Castle, five hours later.

"What's going on, Mike?" Phil asked, when they were on their third pint. "You've been getting jumpier and jumpier over the last few weeks."

"I don't know," Mike said. "Maybe I'm working too hard. Job insecurity doesn't help, either."

"We're all in that boat," Phil said. "But there's something else. Are you going to tell me, or am I going to drag it out of you?"

Reluctantly, Mike met Phil's gaze. He hated to lie, but had no choice.

"There's nothing to tell," he said.

Phil bought them another pint. Mike was starting to feel tired.

"Cynthia," Phil said, slamming the drinks on the table so that the froth dripped over the side.

"A joke," Mike muttered.

"A pretty repetitive joke," Phil stated. "Do you know how many times I've picked up the phone over the last three or four weeks and it's been hung up?"

"You mentioned once or twice," Mike replied.

He had no idea how often Rachel phoned him and didn't get through. He knew of four, maybe five times. He'd told Phil that he'd answered a similar number of silent calls himself.

"Every other day," Phil said. "Twice, one day. I started keeping a record, out of curiosity – notches on the phone book. Do you know how many there are?"

Mike shook his head.

"Twenty. I've been waiting for you to tell me about it. You know what hurts?"

"What?" Mike asked, reluctantly.

"It's not that you don't tell me about it. I mean, that's up to you. No, what hurts is you think that I'm such an idiot I won't notice what's going on."

"I'm sorry," Mike said, slowly. "I don't think that."

"So are you going to tell me?"

"Believe me," Mike said, dejectedly. "I would if I could."

"She's married, then?"

"No. It's not that."

Mike dredged his tired brain for some explanation which would satisfy Phil.

"You know what Tracey reckons?" Phil said. "She reckons that you must be knocking off a school girl."

Mike felt like the truth must be etched all over his face. Luckily, Phil wasn't looking at him. He was supping his drink.

"Where'd she get that idea?" Mike said, trying to sound casual.

"The Cynthia phone call, for one. And opportunity. You hardly go out. When you're not at school, you're thinking about school. If you're not seeing a married teacher, then it can only be a pupil. Makes sense, doesn't it?"

Mike agreed that it made sense. They'd both nearly finished their drinks and it was his turn to buy another one. He felt very tired, and didn't really want it. Yet he needed time to think. Without speaking, he took their glasses to the bar.

"What's that blonde called?" Phil asked when he returned. "The busty one we saw at Rock City with Rachel and Carmen. She's in your year-eleven group."

"You mean Becky."

"Right. Now I have to confess that if I weren't with Tracey, and I came upon her in a club or a wine bar, I wouldn't think twice about ... you know."

Mike nodded, knowing what he was being drawn into.

Phil became less articulate. "Not that I'm saying ... The point is, you can trust me."

"Thanks," Mike said. "I appreciate that, I do. Thing is, I think I know who the phone calls are coming from, and it's not a school kid."

Phil looked surprised. "Who is it then?"

"I think it's my ex, Emma."

"Why would it be her?"

Mike launched into a long, rambling explanation. He said that Emma had always been a bit neurotic. She might have changed her mind about him. Maybe she wanted to keep tabs on Mike because she couldn't stand the thought of him with another woman. It wasn't very convincing, but Phil listened patiently. Mike couldn't tell if he believed him or not.

Thirteen

Rachel finally got to see her father ten days before *Romeo and Juliet* opened. He picked her up from a Saturday morning rehearsal at school and drove her back to Mapperley Park. Rachel looked at the city from the high seats of his Shogun. Dad made an effort to be cheerful but his face was gaunt, his eyes tired. They quickly fell into silence.

"Are you coming to my play?" Rachel asked, as they turned up Tavistock Drive.

"Of course. How long's it on for?"

"Tuesday to Thursday."

"Which night would you like me to come?"

"Mum's bought tickets for the Wednesday."

Dad took the hint. "How about if I come on Thursday, then? You'll have enough first night jitters without me there."

"Fine," Rachel said. "I think there's a party afterwards, so you won't mind if I don't ..."

"No, no," Dad said. "I just want to see you perform."

"So I'll get you two tickets."

Dad frowned. "Better make it one. Clarissa will have to babysit."

For some obscure reason, Rachel was hurt. Despite the fact that they didn't get on, Clarissa generally pretended to be interested in Rachel. Couldn't they afford to pay a babysitter?

"You may have gathered," Dad said, staring at the road ahead as he spoke, "Clarissa and I have been going through a rough patch lately. That's why I've had to keep cancelling things."

"Are you splitting up?" Rachel asked, without looking at him. Dad kept his gaze on the road ahead. "No, no. We're getting over it. You know, most couples have periods in their marriages where ..." He ran out of words.

"Like you and Mum?" Rachel suggested, in a neutral voice.

"Yes," Dad admitted. "Like me and your mother. But I'm not going to make that mistake again."

Rachel expected him to add "for the sake of the children", or some platitude like that, but he didn't.

"Anyway," he said. "Don't mention any of this to Clarissa today. And try to be nice to her. You know, she finds you awfully frosty sometimes."

"I'll try," Rachel said, though she didn't know why she ought to. Wasn't Clarissa the one who was putting her father through hell?

"Your sixteenth birthday is coming up soon," Dad said, as they got out of the car. "Have a think about what you want me to get you."

"I'll do that," Rachel said.

She didn't know what she wanted to do on her birthday, which was on the final Sunday of the Easter holiday. What Rachel really cared about was the night before, when she and Mike were going to see Oasis in Sheffield. Now it occurred to her that Dad might provide the ideal alibi for that night.

"I'll tell you what," she said. "Why don't you invite me for lunch on my birthday?"

She would tell Mum that she was spending the night before at her Dad's.

"Fine," Dad said, "if that's what you want. Present?"

"I'll let you know."

Rachel had intended to ask for a CD player. But if she was going to move in with Mike during the summer, there wasn't much point. He already had one.

Lunch with Dad and Clarissa was rather stiff and formal. Afterwards, Phoebe and Rowan kept Rachel entertained. When Clarissa got back from shopping, Rachel said she wanted to go for a walk on her own, even though it was raining. She rang Mike from a phone box on Mansfield Road. He was expecting Phil home any minute, so he arranged to meet her for a drink in the Grosvenor, a pub just down the road from her Dad's.

Rachel got there first. Mike arrived two minutes later. He looked around before acknowledging Rachel. When Mike sat down, he leant over and kissed her lightly on the lips. The couple were unlikely to be spotted in the loud, crowded pub. Still, they didn't dare draw attention to themselves by being too affectionate.

"Drink?"

Rachel asked for an orange juice, knowing that Mike would be uncomfortable buying her anything alcoholic, even though she looked old enough.

"I liked that LP you taped me," Mike said. "There's some really catchy stuff on it. I tried to get tickets for the concert, but it was sold out." He paused to let Rachel register disappointment, then added, "It wouldn't have been safe to go, really. Going to a gig in Sheffield's one thing, but Nottingham ..."

Rachel nodded. She understood. Mike changed the subject.

"I won't be in school a week on Tuesday," he said.

"But what about the play?"

Tuesday was the opening night.

"I'll be back for that. Thing is, I've got a job interview."

"Where?"

"A school in Sheffield, with a sixth form."

Rachel tried to smile, but she felt like her world was on the verge of falling apart. If he went, could she follow? And would Mike really want her with him?

"Does Ms Howard know?" she asked, putting off the real question.

"I only got the letter today. I'll tell her on Monday."

"W-what about us?" she stuttered. "If you get the job?" Mike squeezed her hand across the table. His voice was reassuring. "I haven't got the job yet. I don't want you to worry about it. There's the play, and then your exams. You know, you need to concentrate more on ..."

"Hello, there."

Rachel and Mike both turned round as though a gun had gone off. Rachel's maths teacher stood over them, his tall body leaning against the table. He wasn't smiling.

"You must be Cynthia," he said.

Rachel froze, then turned to Mike. His face had become a blank – he couldn't seem to focus on Phil Hansen. The pause seemed to last an eternity. Hansen was about to say something else, when Mike suddenly put on his friendly but fake, diplomatic school teacher's voice.

"If you could just give us a minute, Phil. Then I'll explain."

"Sure."

Phil went to the bar. Rachel looked at Mike. His face was now completely white.

168

"I'd better go back to my Dad's," Rachel told him. "Can I call you?"

Mike sighed. "You might as well," he said. "It makes no difference, now he knows."

Her head swimming, Rachel kissed him on the cheek, picked up her umbrella and went. At the door, she glanced back at Mike. Phil Hansen was walking over to him, two pints in his hand. He glanced at Rachel with a sad, subdued look in his eyes. The corners of his mouth curled, but failed to become a smile. As Rachel left the pub, she nearly bumped into a familiar-looking girl with a blonde bob: Phil's girlfriend, Tracey. There was a glow coming from her face like a million dollars. *Why can't I be like that?* Rachel asked herself, although she already knew the answer.

Phil shook his head with barely disguised disgust.

"You bloody idiot," he said.

Tracey arrived and Phil said something to her. She went to the bar alone.

"How long's this been going on?" Phil asked Mike.

"A few weeks."

"Does anyone know?"

Mike thought about Paul Wilks. So far, he seemed to have kept his mouth shut. "No. Only you."

"It's impossible to keep this kind of thing quiet for long."

"Maybe."

"You'd better stop it."

"I can't," Mike said. "I love her."

Tracey joined them but didn't join in the conversation. Now that the secret was out, Mike wanted to unburden himself. He gave a brief account of how he and Rachel got together, how he was even thinking about living with her once they'd both left Stonywood. "I'm sorry," he finished. "I really didn't want to lie to either of you, but I felt like I had no choice. I hoped you'd understand."

Phil remained silent. Tracey gave Mike a sceptical look. "A friend of mine had a thing with her maths teacher when she was in the sixth form," she said. "He had three kids. I guess this isn't as bad as that."

"What happened to her?" Mike asked.

"She dropped out of school, got a job where I work."

"And him?"

"Nothing. He's still at the school, still with his wife. That's what usually happens to blokes like you, isn't it?"

Stung by this criticism, Mike repeated, "I love her."

"Yeah. That's what this bloke said. She believed him. But what do you know about love at sixteen? Oh, sorry – yours is younger, isn't she?"

Mike cringed. Tracey was only eighteen herself. She ought to be sympathetic, he thought, but said nothing.

"Trace," Phil said. "Have a heart."

Tracey's blue eyes flashed angrily as she turned to Phil.

"A *heart*? I said, didn't I, that this would be what was going on. And you're going to help protect him, aren't you? Well, you can leave me out of it." Without finishing her drink, she walked out of the pub. Phil didn't try and stop her. He raised a withering eyebrow at Mike.

"Thanks a lot, mate," he said.

Mike didn't know what to say. "I really love her," he mumbled.

Phil's voice was scathing. "She's just a kid. I know Rachel. I teach her three times a week. I don't understand ..."

"We have a lot in common," Mike protested. "She's intelligent. She's articulate. She's ..."

"... not very good at maths," Phil filled in. "And she's lazy, like a lot of kids her age who think they know it all. You got a first class honours degree, didn't you?"

Mike nodded.

"Well, Rachel won't even get into university."

Mike began to protest. "I don't see how ..."

Phil shook his head. "You need maths GCSE at C or above to get into university. Rachel's left it too late to get that. She'll only get a D if she works for it."

"She's going to go to college next year," Mike insisted. "She can retake it there. Anyway, what is this – a parents' evening? I don't ask you what exam results Tracey got."

"Leave Tracey out of this," Phil ordered. "She hated school, messed up, got out as soon as she could."

"What have you got against Rachel?" Mike asked. "Apart from her being bad at maths?"

Phil gave Mike a withering look. "I like Rachel. It's you I'm down on. I thought you were my friend."

"I am," Mike insisted. "This isn't so bad. All we have to do is keep it quiet for a few more months. I'll get a new job, she'll move in with me and ..."

"And what?" Phil asked. "Rachel will become a nice little housewife? No way. She might not get to university, but she'll want to make something of her life and she'll leave you behind, mate. And you'll be even more bitter and mixed up than you were when Emma dumped you."

Mike saw what he was getting at. "You think I'm doing all this on the rebound, don't you?"

Phil shrugged. "Something like that, maybe. You're under a lot of pressure. I can see how it happened. Rachel got a crush on you. You were flattered. You flirted a bit. You know, I can see the attraction. In a couple of years,

Rachel will be a knock out. But she's too young, Mike. You have to stop seeing her."

"I can't do that."

Phil stood up. "Then more fool you. And I don't want you seeing her in my house. I mean that. If it gets out, I could end up in trouble, too. I don't want to lose my job if I can help it, thanks very much."

Mike didn't reply. He didn't want to make a promise which he knew he wouldn't be able to keep. Phil pulled on his coat.

"I'm going off to find Tracey."

"I'll give you a lift," Mike offered.

"No thanks," Phil replied. "I prefer to walk."

Fourteen

Opening night arrived. Rachel hadn't seen Mike on his own in the ten days since Phil caught them together in the pub. She'd spoken to him on the phone, though, using a call box near her house. He'd told her not to worry, Mr Hansen would keep quiet. Even so, Rachel hadn't been able to look the maths teacher in the eye during lessons. It all felt wrong: his knowing ought to make her feel more grown up. Instead, it made Rachel feel like a child with a shameful secret.

The play dominated everything. The dress rehearsal was on Monday, and went OK. However, there was to be a teachers' strike on Tuesday, the day they opened. The school was closed. Ms Howard had everyone involved with the play come in anyway, to go over the rough patches one more time. The teachers who weren't on strike could be seen hanging around the empty school, looking guilty. Mike, however, didn't have to choose between the strike and the play. He had his interview.

Ms Howard hurried around, harassing everybody. Yesterday, the lights had been a disaster. Several had blown. She'd had a man in all this afternoon checking them and finally seemed satisfied. Now she was going over the blocking with Rachel.

"Remember, the sightlines during the dance scene are very narrow. You mustn't get carried away."

It was an hour before the performance. They were in the

girls' dressing room, across a corridor from the boys' one. There was a knock on the door and a familiar voice called, "Everyone decent?"

Rachel heaved a sigh of relief. Mike walked in, still wearing his best jacket. She wanted to ask how he'd got on, but wasn't supposed to know where he'd been.

Ms Howard gave him a grumpy look. "Any joy?" she asked.

Mike shook his head. "I was runner up. The internal candidate got it."

"Bad luck," Ms Howard murmured, unconvincingly.

Rachel was relieved. She hadn't wanted Mike to move back to Sheffield. What she really wanted was for him to get a job somewhere else in Nottingham. That way, they could see each other easily and move in together when they chose to, not when circumstances dictated. Rachel gave her boy-friend the smallest of affectionate glances. He turned quickly away.

"I'll get to the boys' dressing room," he said. "Good luck everybody."

The play was Mike's first involvement in a school production, so he had nothing to compare it to. Nick made a pretty good Romeo, but there was something missing in his relationship with Juliet – you never really got the sense that they were crazy about each other. Rachel was adequate, though her voice disappeared at times. The supporting cast were mixed. Only Troy Martin, as Friar Lawrence, had a real presence. The set was too sparse. The lighting was all over the place, and the pauses between scenes were almost unbearable. By the end of the evening, Mike had decided that you needed a sixth form to do Shakespeare properly.

But maybe he was being too critical. The Head described the evening as a triumph. Mrs Perry even came on at the end, after the curtain call, to praise the cast – and Judith Howard – to the skies. Mike, and the other teachers who'd helped, weren't mentioned by name.

Mike managed to contrive to take several of the cast home, including Nick and Rachel. He went a roundabout way to ensure that he dropped Rachel off last. Finally, they were alone together for the first time in ten days. Mike parked at the end of her street.

"What did you *really* think?" she asked.

They had important things to discuss, but all Rachel wanted to talk about was the play.

"You were fine," he said, "except for a few points where I couldn't hear you."

"Yeah. Ms Howard mentioned them."

"The main thing was, it could have done with more passion."

"It's hard to fake passion," Rachel said.

"It's called acting," Mike said, in a light voice, trying not to sound condescending.

"If I hold him too close," Rachel protested, "Nick starts to think that I mean it."

"Let him think what he wants," Mike insisted. "Tomorrow night, kiss him properly."

"You mean like *this*?"

She leant over and pushed her mouth against his. Mike was hungry for her, but couldn't take the risk. He pulled away.

"Not here," he said.

"Where?"

"Next week. Phil and Tracey go away on Tuesday."

There were people walking by the car, he realized: young people. They could be on their way back from the school.

"You'd better get out now," he said.

Rachel opened the car door and did as she was told.

"Goodnight, sir," she said, loudly. "Thanks for the lift."

Mike shivered for a second or two, then drove away.

Rachel lay on her tomb, listening as the play unfolded around her. Romeo killed his rival, Paris. Then, seeing Juliet's lifeless body next to that of Tybalt, he took poison and killed himself. Tonight, Nick and Rachel had gelled better. Rachel was glad, because her mum was in the audience. She got ready to wake. Next, Friar Lawrence came in and saw the dead bodies. Rachel got up, and spoke her words.

"O comfortable Friar! Where is my lord?"

The friar told her and Rachel sent him away. She didn't like her last lines in the play much. Romeo got so many great speeches, but she was left with a few pitiful words, berating the man she'd lost for having left Juliet no poison to kill herself with. Rachel wanted a tragic speech, not this teenage tantrum.

Tenderly, she leant down and kissed Nick. Then the watchman made a noise outside. Rachel picked up Romeo's knife.

"O happy dagger!
This is thy sheath; there rust, and let me die."

As she pressed it against her breast, a blood-balloon burst and Rachel fell to the floor. She had five long minutes on the hard stage as the families appeared and learnt what had happened. Then it was over.

Tonight's applause was louder and warmer than the night

before, and there was no embarrassing speech from the Head. Nick and Rachel held hands as they took a second curtain call, then smiled warmly at each other as they walked off stage.

"Walk you home?" Nick offered. "It's a nice night."

"Sorry," Rachel told him. "My mum's here."

As she hurried into the dressing room, Mike put an arm around Rachel's shoulder.

"Well done. You were brilliant."

Rachel gave him her most dazzling smile, but Mike turned away and missed it. He was speaking to Nick. "You too, Nick. Well done."

Mum was equally impressed. When they hugged, it was the first time they'd been close to each other for a few weeks. As they were leaving, Ms Howard's advised Rachel to take the next day off school in order to rest up for the final performance.

"I've said the same to Nick. I know how much energy all this takes up."

Then Mike was by the door, in sweater and jeans. Mum didn't recognize him at first. Rachel hoped he wouldn't offer them a lift. He didn't.

"Wasn't that your English teacher?" Mum asked, as they walked into the cool, night air. "Is he involved in the play?"

"He did a lot in rehearsal," Rachel told her. "He helped me with my lines."

"Funny," Mum said. "I don't remember you mentioning that before."

Fifteen

Having the day off school didn't help Rachel relax. Still, the final performance of the play went nearly as well as the night before. Mr Hansen was there, using the school video camera to make a record of it. This made Rachel even more nervous than usual, but she didn't fluff too many lines.

Dad was in the audience, as were Carmen and Becky. He waited for her afterwards.

"You were tremendous," he said. "I was really proud of you."

"Thanks," Rachel said. "That means a lot."

Becky bounded over. "Carmen had to go," she explained. "She said to say that you were excellent. I thought so, too. You know, I was wrong about you and Nick – you made a really convincing couple."

Then Becky noticed Rachel's father, who was smiling warmly at her.

"Aren't you going to introduce me to your friend, Rachel?"

"Actually," Becky said, "we've met before, years ago. I'm Becky."

As Dad chatted to Becky, Rachel caught Mike's shoulder. "Are you coming to the party, sir?" she asked.

"For a few minutes," he said. "But I have to give Mr Hansen a lift home."

"How about you, Becky?" Rachel offered. "There's a

bit of a party back stage for the cast and friends."

"Why not?" Becky said.

Rachel kissed her father goodbye.

The party wasn't much of a party. Being at school, there was no alcohol. It was mainly an excuse for people to let their hair down now that the play was over. Nick had made a tape, which he put on. The music was too trendy for most of the cast, but a few kids danced anyway. Mr Hansen played around with the video camera, trying to get embarrassing shots of everyone. Ms Howard watched indulgently from a corner of the room.

"Dance with me?" Rachel said to Mike, finding him near the tape machine.

"I'm not sure ..." Mike's expression said he thought it was a bad idea.

"For a minute or two," Rachel insisted. "C'mon. That's what young teachers are meant to do."

"I guess."

Nervously, Mike gyrated to Blur's "Girls and Boys", a song Rachel didn't like. As Phil pointed the video camera in their direction, Becky blocked his view.

"Put that camera down and start dancing," she ordered the maths teacher. Phil Hansen did as he was told. Soon after the song was over, however, he and Mike left the party. They said abrupt goodnights to the cast and teachers.

"I guess it's time for us to go, too," Rachel told Becky.

Nick, she saw, was being chatted up by Marie Foulks. Rachel wanted to say goodnight to him, but felt awkward about it. She and Becky walked home through light rain.

"It's ages since we've had a proper talk," Becky said.

"The play's over now," Rachel told her. "Things'll be different."

"Is the play all that's over?" Becky asked.

Rachel answered uncomfortably. "You mean ...?"

"Your mysterious boyfriend."

"He's back at university," Rachel said, wishing that she didn't have to lie, not tonight, when she was feeling so elated.

"No, he's not," Becky said. "You were dancing with him ten minutes ago."

Rachel stopped cold. "Pardon?"

Becky gave Rachel her old, no-nonsense stare. "I guessed weeks ago," she said. "But tonight confirmed it – the way he didn't want to dance with you, and Mr Hansen dragged him home as soon as the song was over. He knows, too, doesn't he?"

Rachel stared at the pavement and nodded.

"In which case," Becky said, "I think that the least you can do is to tell me all about it."

They went to Becky's bedroom and talked. There was no need to swear Becky to secrecy. She was Rachel's oldest friend and it was a relief to tell her.

"You said you knew ages ago," Rachel said when she'd finished. "How?"

Becky gave her a slightly patronizing smile. "You had this *glow* about you," she said. "I could tell how you were feeling – it was like me and Gary last summer. And I knew it wasn't just a one-afternoon stand. There had to be a reason why you weren't telling me about it. You had to be seeing someone you shouldn't."

"But Mr Steadman? I mean, Mike?"

Becky shrugged. "Once I figured it must be a teacher, it could only be one of two. I thought it was Mr Hansen, but then I kept noticing the way Steadman looks at you when he thinks no one's watching. At first, I thought it was me he was eyeing up. But I caught you sneaking looks at him, too."

"Is it that obvious?" Rachel asked, concerned.

Becky shook her head. "Only to me, I think."

"I'm relieved," Rachel said. She asked the biggest question on her mind. "But what do you think?"

"You know what we used to say," Becky told her. "Only idiots get crushes on their teachers."

"This is more than a crush," Rachel insisted.

"So you told me," Becky said.

The two girls burst into giggles.

"It's the best bit of gossip I've heard all year," Becky said when they'd stopped, "and I can't tell anyone. Do you know how frustrating that is?"

"I can imagine."

"So what are you going to do next?"

Rachel told her about the Oasis concert. "After that, we'll have to play it very quietly. Hopefully, Mike will get a new job lined up. But there's also the exams. I'm way behind."

"So I've noticed. At first, I thought it was just to do with the play. Still, it's not too late. We said we were going to revise for English and History together, remember?"

"Let's do that," Rachel said.

It was getting late. Becky saw Rachel to the door.

"Do you think what we're doing is wrong?" Rachel asked.

Becky met Rachel's gaze. Rachel saw sympathy in her eyes, but no sign of a judgement. "Who knows what's right or wrong?" Becky asked. "I mean, if you really love each other... But it's dangerous. He might lose his job and you..."

"Yes?"

Becky thought for a moment. "You'll probably be all right," she said. "But be very careful."

"I am being."

Rachel walked home in the pouring rain, relieved that she'd told Becky. The rain didn't matter. The play had been a triumph. Mike loved her. Becky was still her best friend, and the Easter holidays started tomorrow. Even Mum, when Rachel came in late, didn't complain about the time, or her walking home alone, but poured them both a drink to celebrate the end of the play. For the first time in weeks, Rachel fell asleep quickly, not worrying about anything.

Sixteen

The Easter holidays were a honeymoon. With Phil and Tracey away and Mum at work, Rachel and Mike could see almost as much of each other as they wanted. And there was the concert to look forward to. Mum was disappointed that Rachel would be away from home on the night before her birthday, but could hardly deny Dad his half of her day.

She and Mike drove to Sheffield and parked on a side street, then walked to the Arena. There were coaches outside from places as far away as Plymouth and Scotland. It was Rachel's first gig and she was full of anticipation. Mike told her that she looked great. Walking in with him, Rachel felt proud and not at all out of place, like part of a real couple.

"Uh-oh," Mike muttered.

"What is it?" Rachel asked.

A woman of about twenty was coming away from one of the food stalls. She was with an older man in a leather jacket. The woman noticed Mike and Rachel. For a fleeting moment, she seemed uneasy. Then her lips became a pout. She gave Rachel a cool, appraising look. Rachel took an instant dislike to her.

"Hello, Mike," the woman said, in a neutral voice. "How are you?"

"Fine," Mike said. "This is Rachel. Rachel, Emma, and Steve."

Rachel smiled at the woman.

"Nice to meet you," Emma said, with an odd look.

The man nodded, with a fierce frown, but didn't speak.

"Let's find our seats," Emma said.

As he walked past Mike, Steve grunted something which Mike didn't react to. So, Rachel thought, that was Emma. She didn't look anything special. For a second, she worried that they would be sitting next to them. But, no, Mike explained, he'd bought all the tickets, but hadn't been able to get four seats together. He and Rachel had the better ones.

They found their seats. Mike and Rachel were in the raised side tiers on the right of the stage. There was a gap between them and the main body of the hall, which was in two all-standing sections, where people could dance. It was like being at a huge house party. The "no smoking" signs were being ignored and half the crowd seemed to be high on something. Rachel felt high on life itself.

The lights dimmed. Mike gripped her hand. Music boomed out of the PA. Rachel recognized an old Beatles' song, from *Yellow Submarine*. The song was followed by another from the same album, "It's All Too Much". Then the Arena went completely dark. Oasis took the stage. A year ago, they hadn't had a record out. Now they were the biggest band in the country. It was like a fairy tale and Rachel felt part of it. The music began.

As Oasis launched into "Rock'n'Roll Star", the crowd went wild. Rachel jumped up and down. She would have liked more room to dance, like the crowd in the standing area. There was something strange about the standing area, though. The bigger, back section was crowded. The smaller front section, partitioned off with wooden barriers, was less than half full, even now. Rachel asked Mike why.

"They can't have more people standing than would normally sit there," he explained, between songs. "Fire regulations, or something."

The band seemed to agree. Before the third number, the singer complained about the empty space. As the group launched into their new single, a tide of people swept across the other side of the Arena, knocked over the barriers and began to climb into the front section. The house lights came up, but the band played on.

Then the surge began on their side. People from the back standing section vaulted the wooden barriers, then ran down the alley to the front. People from the side tiers by Mike and Rachel jumped down into the alley and followed them.

"Come on!" Rachel said to Mike.

"It might be dangerous," he said, in his teacher's voice.

People were helping each other over the wooden barriers. The floor was now a mass of wild, exuberant bodies. Security staff ran around like frightened farm animals, not knowing how to regain control. Rachel wanted to take her chance before they succeeded. She turned to Mike.

"I'm going. I want to dance."

Rachel jumped the four or five feet to the floor. Reluctantly, Mike joined her. They ran to the front. A security guard grabbed at Rachel, but she shook him off. Then Mike helped her over the barrier, and they were in.

The house lights stayed on, even when security was restored. The front section was now a thronging mosh pit, but there was no crush. During the acoustic set, everyone stopped throwing themselves against each other and held lighters aloft. Rachel felt like she'd died and gone to heaven. Oasis ended the set with her favourite Beatles' song, "I am the Walrus". Rachel, elated, sang along with every word.

All the way home, Rachel couldn't stop talking about the gig. They got back at midnight, both incredibly aroused. The moment she and Mike walked into the house, they began to undress each other. They had sex in the living room, on the sofa, on the floor, against the front door. It was stupendous. Rachel never knew that it could be like this. It was like a continuation of the concert: like they were throwing themselves over the edge without looking down.

When they were finished, there were books, videos and other debris strewn across the carpet. They didn't bother to clear up, but went for a shower and made love again in the bathroom. Still wide awake, they tidied up, played music and talked. Then they went to bed and began again: more slowly and passionately this time.

"What time of day were you born?" Mike asked, afterwards, pulling the curtains closed as the first light of dawn shimmered beneath the clouds.

"Eight in the morning, I think."

"Then next time we make love, it'll be legal."

"It better not put you off me," Rachel teased him.

They drifted to sleep, naked in each other's arms.

It was afternoon when they woke. Mike made a pot of tea and gave Rachel the white linen dress he'd bought for her birthday.

"I love you," he said, giving it to her. "I want to spend the rest of my life with you."

Rachel hugged him and tried the dress on. It looked wonderful. Mike caressed her. They both wanted to make love again, but she was already late for her father's. Reluctantly, Rachel left her gift behind in Mike's wardrobe.

Mike drove her to Mapperley Park. On the way, they chatted unselfconsciously, like two people who knew each other better than anyone else in the world. Rachel was only twenty minutes late. Her alibi wasn't in much danger: Dad was hardly likely to have phoned Mum to check where she was. He hated phoning Mum.

As Rachel was about to get out of the car, Mike stroked her arm, then gave her a warning. "Remember what we agreed. For the next few weeks, we have to knock it on the head, not give anyone reason to suspect. And you have to revise."

"I know," Rachel said, wishing that Mike didn't have to come on like a school teacher just now. Who could think about exams at a time like this?

"I love you," he repeated. "Happy birthday."

"I love you," she said, softly kissing him one last time. "I always will."

Then she got out of the car and walked to her father's house.

Rachel hadn't seen Dad since the play, two and a half weeks before. She'd told him that she wanted money for her present. How much, she wondered, walking in, would he give her? It was a warm, sunny day. Rowan and Phoebe were playing in the garden. Rachel waved at them and both children called excitedly. They couldn't run up to her, because the garden gate was kept locked. You could only get to the garden through the conservatory.

Rachel rang the front doorbell. She had a long wait before Clarissa answered it.

"Rachel!"

Clarissa had her hair tied back, and wore an old tracksuit. She looked worn out.

"Sorry I'm late," Rachel said. "I ..."

"What are you doing here?" Clarissa asked, blocking the door so that Rachel couldn't come in.

"For lunch. It's my birthday. I ..."

Clarissa was shaking her head. "I can't believe he didn't tell you ..." she said.

"Tell me what?"

Clarissa took a deep breath. "Eric doesn't live here any more. We've split up."

Rachel stared in shock at her father's second wife. Then she turned and looked at the children playing in the garden. She didn't know what to say.

"How ... did it happen?" she found herself asking Clarissa.

"I think it's for your father to tell you that."

Rachel blinked. She could tell that she was about to cry. A moment ago, her heart had been filled with tenderness and love for everything in the world. But now, an old bitter feeling shot to the front of her head and she knew that it had been there all along, hiding, waiting to take control when the tide changed.

"I'd like to hear it from you," she told Clarissa. "Can I come in?"

Clarissa shook her head. She looked like she wanted to slam the door in Rachel's face. "I don't think so."

The two women stared at each other for a few moments. *She's kicked him out*, Rachel decided. *That's why she can't face me. Maybe she's even got someone else in there.*

Clarissa spoke again. "You've got keys to this place, haven't you? I'd like them back, please. I've already taken Eric's. I don't want to go to the expense of changing all the locks."

Without thinking, Rachel took the keys from her pocket

and handed them over. "How can you do this?" she said to Clarissa. "To Dad, to Phoebe and Rowan? You don't know what it's like, growing up without a father around ..."

Clarissa's face reddened. "You know nothing, Rachel. Do you hear me? Nothing! Ask your father."

This time, she did slam the door in Rachel's face.

Rachel stood there, in silence, for several seconds. When she looked around, Phoebe and Rowan were standing on the other side of the locked garden gate, staring at her.

"Are you coming to play, Rachel?" Phoebe asked.

Rowan had a small yellow kaleidoscope in his hands. Rachel had given it to him for his last birthday. She used to make up bedtime stories about how it had strange, magic powers. Now Rowan poked it through the cast-iron gate, inviting Rachel to take it, to tell another one. From inside the house, the children's mother called them.

"Are you coming?" Phoebe repeated.

Rachel couldn't stop the tears welling up in her eyes. She leant forward and squeezed the children's tiny hands on the other side of the dark, locked gate.

"Not today," she said, softly, tasting salt water as she spoke. "I'm sorry. Not today."

Clarissa called again. Through blurred eyes, Rachel saw the children's bewildered faces. Then she ran up the path, out on to the road and turned down the street which Mike had driven her up less than five minutes before.

"Good Easter?" Phil asked, when he'd finished describing his Greek island holiday. He'd arrived home, deeply suntanned, while Mike was taking Rachel to her father's.

"Pretty good."

"See much of Rachel?"

Without answering directly, Mike launched into a blow-by-blow account of the concert the night before. He didn't mention seeing Emma, or the barbed comment about Rachel that her brother made before walking away: "School outing, is it?"

"And where did Rachel's mother think she was?" Phil asked.

"At her father's. Her parents don't talk to each other."

Phil gave Mike a censurious look. "You know, Trace and I talked about this a lot on holiday. I persuaded Trace that she'd been a bit hard on you."

"Thanks," Mike said, grudgingly.

"But we both agreed," Phil went on, "you have to stop seeing her outside school – at least until Rachel finishes her exams and you've got another job. More for your sake than hers, though seeing you can hardly be helping with her school work. If you get found out ..."

"You don't have to rub it in," Mike said. "Rachel and I agreed this morning – we're knocking it on the head until the summer."

"Maybe you'll both have grown out of it by then," Phil added.

"I doubt it," Mike told him. "I doubt it very much." He changed the subject. "What about you and Tracey? Are you moving in together?"

Phil nodded. "We were together twenty-four hours a day for ten days. I've never managed that with anyone before. We never got bored with each other. Even when we ran out of things to say, the silences were comfortable. Do you know what I mean?"

"I think so," Mike said. He pictured himself and Rachel on holiday abroad. For a moment, it seemed real.

It was two-thirty when Rachel got back to Stonywood. She'd needed to recover herself, to work out how to explain to Mum that she'd spent the night in Mapperley Park, but hadn't seen her father. She needn't have bothered. When Rachel got to her street, there was a police panda parked outside the house.

The front door was ajar, so Rachel walked quietly in. She could hear the policewoman's voice from the narrow hall.

"We spoke to one of the friends whose name you gave us. She was very vague, but thought she'd heard Rachel mention that she might be going to a concert last night."

"Who with?" Mum asked.

"Some lad whose name she claimed not to know. That's the most likely explanation, I assure you. With girls her age, it happens all the time."

Rachel wanted to leave, but resisted the urge. She opened the living-room door to face the music.

"I'm sorry," she told her mother. "I didn't mean to worry you. I thought if I said I was at Dad's . . ."

She collapsed into an armchair. The police officer gave Rachel a lecture, but Rachel didn't listen to it. She hadn't had enough sleep and felt exhausted. When the woman had gone, Mum sat down opposite her.

"Your father rang at six last night," she told Rachel. "He said that there were unforeseen circumstances and he'd have to cancel lunch today. I've been going out of my mind ever since. Where were you?"

"I went to a gig, in Sheffield."

"I'm not sure I believe you, Rachel. All this deceit for a concert?"

Rachel produced the ticket, her proud souvenir. She

handed it to Mum, who checked the date, then tore it into tiny pieces. Rachel didn't protest.

"And where were you since then?"

"At this boy's place."

"He has his own place?"

"Yes."

"And a car. And he can buy you expensive concert tickets. He's quite a catch, isn't he?"

"I love him," Rachel whispered.

Mum came over. She gripped Rachel's shoulders and began to shake them. "Then why can't I meet him? Why don't you tell me who he is? Can't you see how worrying this is for me? I'm imagining a criminal, one of those long-haired people with dogs you see on the streets. I'm imagining someone who's giving you dangerous drugs. I don't mind if you're sleeping with him. You're not under age any more. It's your decision. But I need to know that you're safe."

"I'm safe," Rachel said, quietly.

"Then why can't I meet him?" Mum pleaded. "Why can't you at least tell me who he is? Is he married?"

"He's not married," Rachel told her. "And he's not a criminal either. You can't meet him because, because . . . he has to go away for a while, on work. And I want to concentrate on my exams. When he comes back, you can meet him then."

Mum looked at Rachel with undisguised distrust and concern. Rachel wanted to tell her about Clarissa, but couldn't. Mum never wanted to know about Clarissa.

"Did Dad say anything else?" she asked.

"He said he'd call to make sure that you're all right, but he wouldn't be able to see you for a while. Reading between the lines, I think he's split up with number two."

"Yes," Rachel said, but didn't add anything further. "I want to go to bed for a bit now. I'm very tired."

"All right," Mum told her, resignedly.

Suddenly, Rachel threw her arms around her mother. "I don't like having secrets," she said. "I do love you, Mum. I'm sorry I scared you."

"Rachel," Mum said, stroking her daughter's hair, "you scare me more and more all the time. But I love you, too. I'm here when you're ready to talk. Remember that."

"Thanks," Rachel told her, taking the tissue Mum offered to wipe her eyes. She turned to go up to her bedroom.

"By the way," Mum said, "happy birthday."

Part Three

One

It was a fine spring. There were four weeks of term before study leave began. Mike's year-eleven group had finished all their coursework. Now they had two exams to prepare for. Mike kept giving them practice papers, creating huge mounds of marking for himself. He didn't mind. The harder he worked, the more he kept himself from missing Rachel. They talked on the phone two or three times a week, but it wasn't easy, seeing each other all the time without being able to see each other properly.

Mike applied for jobs, but there weren't many about. Most of the ones he found in the *Times Educational Supplement* were in the south of the country, where he knew no one and it was expensive to live. He couldn't afford to take Rachel with him and support her on a schoolteacher's pay.

What did Rachel want? The redundancies would be announced soon. Mike didn't know if he was on the list. Judith Howard said he wouldn't be. If that was true, Mike had to make a decision. What did he want most: a job, or Rachel? Mike wished that he could talk things over with his girlfriend, but it wouldn't be fair. Rachel had other things on her mind. He didn't want to burden her with hypotheticals about the future.

One week, Mike was runner up for a job in Northampton. The next, he withdrew from an interview at a sixth-form college in Wakefield. He'd wanted to teach sixth form, but the conditions of work for lecturers were awful and staff morale non-existent. He couldn't face it. Anyway, if Rachel came with him, they'd come up against the same problem they had at Stonywood – he might be teaching where she studied. Better to stick to schools.

At the beginning of May, Phil moved in with Tracey. Now that Mike had the house to himself, it was harder for him to resist seeing Rachel. When she rang him, early one Wednesday evening, he asked if she could get away.

"I thought we agreed ..."

"I know, but ... I miss you so much."

"Me, too. I'm meant to be revising round at Becky's in half an hour. I'll go round there and explain. Meet me in the usual place at eight."

It was nearly twenty-past when he got Rachel back to the house, and she had to be home by ten. They went straight to bed and, afterwards, Mike was unable to stop himself dozing of. At quarter to ten, Rachel woke him up.

"We have to go soon."

Mike blinked. "I'm sorry. I really wanted to talk."

"It's all right," Rachel assured him. "I enjoyed holding you, watching you sleep. I never normally get to do that."

They dressed and got back into the car.

"What did you tell Becky?" Mike asked Rachel.

"The truth."

"The *truth*?"

Instead of starting the car, he turned to her.

"She guessed," Rachel said. "After the play. I couldn't lie about it."

"How did she guess?" Mike demanded to know.

Rachel looked flustered. "Something about the way we

behave with each other. Guilty looks. That kind of thing. But she won't tell anyone. She promised."

Mike put his head in his hands.

"Two and a half more weeks," Rachel said, wanting to change the subject. "Then I'm on exam leave."

"How's the revision going?" Mike asked, forcing himself to sound casual, but trying to think about the implications of Becky knowing, too.

"You don't want to know," Rachel replied.

Mike still didn't turn the key in the ignition.

"Look," Rachel said, "I know you're upset about Becky, but she's my best friend. One day, I hope she'll be your friend, too. I have to have someone to share things with. After all, you've got Mr ... Phil."

"Not any more I haven't," Mike muttered.

He tried to get his head around being Becky's friend, of him going out with Rachel, Becky and Becky's boyfriend, a travel agent, as a foursome. But he couldn't picture it.

"Mike," Rachel said, "we'd better hurry. I don't want Mum ringing up Becky's house to find out why I'm late. She thinks that my mysterious boyfriend is working abroad, or something."

"Sorry," Mike said. He drove towards the ringroad, his indicator nudging past the speed limit.

"Not so fast," Rachel said. "We don't want to get stopped again."

As they slowed down near Rachel's street, she asked, "When can we see each other again? The weekend?"

"I'd like that," Mike said. "Call me. We'll see if ..." He swore. "Duck!"

Walking down the road towards them were Kate Duerden and Lisa Sharpe. Mike accelerated. Rachel did as she was told. The two girls looked round at the speeding car. Mike prayed that they hadn't recognized his rusty Escort, or its occupants.

"What was all that about?" Rachel asked, when he parked.

Mike told her.

"And did they see us?"

"I've no idea. I doubt it. But we'll have to be even more careful."

Rachel looked at her watch. It was ten-fifteen. "I'd better go."

She squeezed his hand.

"I wish I wasn't your teacher," Mike said.

"But then I wouldn't know you."

Mike sighed. "Yes. That would be worse. But we mustn't meet again, not till the exams are over."

"All right," Rachel said, reluctantly.

She got out of the car without kissing him. It was a mild night, but Mike was sweating and shivering at the same time. In two and a half weeks, he reminded himself, Rachel would have had her last lesson from him. Maybe then he could breathe again.

Two

Rachel waited by the bus stop for Becky. Despite their best intentions, the two girls had found little time to revise together. But it wasn't the exams which were uppermost in Rachel's mind. She was feeling isolated, and badly needed someone to talk to. It had to be Becky. Rachel couldn't talk to Mike, and every conversation with Mum seemed to lead to some kind of row. Maybe, this weekend, they could... Her thoughts were interrupted by a tap on her shoulder.

"You've hardly said a word to me since the play finished." It was Nick.

"I'm sorry," Rachel said. "I've been a bit preoccupied."

"I noticed. I like your haircut by the way. It suits you."

"Thanks," Rachel said, and tried to smile. Despite her boyfriend's misgivings, she'd had her hair cut short the weekend before, Mike had given her a funny look in Monday's lesson, but Rachel hadn't seen him alone since. She didn't know whether he liked it or not.

"There's something I thought I ought to tell you," Nick said.

"What?"

Nick had an odd look on his face – a mixture of embarrassment and concern.

"There's this rumour – I don't know if you've heard it ..."

Rachel shook her head. "About what?"

Nick looked over Rachel's shoulder, making sure that no one was listening.

"About you and Mr Steadman. Some people are saying that you're ..."

"What?"

"Having an affair," Nick said, making the words almost delicate.

Rachel did her best to express incredulity and annoyance. "That's ridiculous! Where do they get it from? Who's saying it?"

"I don't know where it comes from," Nick told her. "But three people have asked me whether I'd heard about it: Marie, Kate, Steve Brown. You know what people are like – they were teasing me because I used to go out with you."

"And what did you tell them?" Rachel asked, sharply.

Nick began to sound angry. "That I thought it was rubbish. I mean, I know Steadman gave you a lift home two or three times, but I was in the car, too, wasn't I?"

"Yes," Rachel said. "That's probably it. People saw me in his car."

"Anyway," Nick went on, "you know how rumours spread. I thought you ought to know."

"Thanks," Rachel said. Head clouded, she searched for something else to say, but could only manage, "I'll be glad when I'm out of this dump."

"Me too," Nick told her. "Have you decided where you're going in the autumn?"

"No," Rachel said. "Clarendon, maybe. Or High Pavement."

She wasn't making a definite decision about sixth-form college until she knew what Mike was doing. He still hadn't got a job for next term. They needed to talk.

"Walk you home?" Nick offered.

"Thanks, but I'm waiting for Becky."

Nick left. Rachel was glad that he hadn't actually asked her if the rumours were true. Nick was her only male friend – whatever that was worth – and she felt guilty that there'd been times when she'd hurt him. Rachel valued Nick's friendship, especially at the moment, when she didn't even know where her own father was.

"Do you know what happened in my year-ten lesson today?" Phil asked Mike on the way home.

"What?"

"Karen Wilks asked me if it was true that you were going out with Rachel Webster."

Mike didn't reply. He was too busy thinking. Karen Wilks must be Paul Wilks' sister. Paul had seen Rachel kiss Mike. But it was a while ago. Even if he had told her something, Paul's sister was unlikely to believe it.

"Funny thing was," Phil carried on, "the way she said it. As if there was nothing wrong with a teacher going out with a pupil – she was just curious."

"What did you tell her?" Mike asked.

"I told her not to be silly," Phil said. "I told her that she shouldn't spread rumours. She told me that it was already all over the school."

Mike swore. "Rachel will have left in a fortnight," he told Phil.

"But year ten won't have," Phil told him. "You've got problems."

"People don't take those kinds of rumours seriously," Mike protested.

"Unless they're true," Phil warned.

Mike let him out at the end of Tracey's street. They made no arrangements to meet at the weekend. Their friendship, Mike realized, was slipping away. Phil was his colleague and landlord now, but not a lot more.

When Mike got home, the phone was ringing. It stopped as he got through the door. That would be Rachel. She was practically the only person who phoned him at home. Mike was glad he'd missed her. He didn't dare meet Rachel this weekend. He didn't dare meet her at all.

Mike picked up the mail which had arrived after he left for work that morning. There was a letter offering him an interview at a sixth-form college in Mansfield. It wasn't a great job, but Mike was glad that he'd applied for it. He needed a way out of Stonywood, fast. He'd be letting Judith down, but he hadn't had a formal job offer for next year yet. They could always get someone else.

Anyway, it wasn't Judith who counted. It was Rachel. If Mike stayed at Stonywood, he couldn't openly go out with her, especially not now that these rumours were circulating. He had been working out a plan whereby, if he kept his job, he and Rachel would pretend to start seeing each other in the summer. They would build the relationship up carefully so that, with luck, Rachel's mother would approve, and no one at school would suspect when the affair really started. But that would no longer wash.

Rachel rang again at six. She couldn't talk for long, she said. She was in a call box and there was already a queue.

"I don't think we can see each other," Mike told her, tenderly. "We agreed."

"There's something you need to know," Rachel interrupted. "People are talking."

"I know. But it's only talk."

"If Kate and Lisa saw us . . ."

"I'll say they were mistaken. As long as we're not seen together again, we'll be all right."

There was a pause before Rachel spoke again. When she did, her voice was like that of a little girl, holding back tears.

"I don't know if I can stand not seeing you at all."

"You'll see me in lessons."

"That's worse."

"We'll manage something," Mike said. "But not for a while."

"Can't I come over this weekend?" Rachel pleaded. "I'll take a taxi. There'll be no chance of anyone seeing."

Mike had to be firm. "No. Once you've left school, and I've got another job lined up, we'll see. Hopefully, that won't be long."

He didn't tell her about the new interview. He didn't want to raise her – or his own – hopes.

"I love you," Rachel said. "It's hard, not being able to hold you."

"Me, too," Mike said, his willpower melting. "Look, maybe we can manage an hour next week, or something. I just . . ."

He could hear someone tapping on the phone box with a coin.

"I've got to go," she said.

Rachel ran out of the phone box in tears. She didn't care who saw. A car hooted as she crossed the road. Rachel charged on. How could he speak to her like that? *We'll see. You'll see me in lessons.* Mike was making her feel like a schoolgirl again, or, worse, a child being patronized by a parent. It was humiliating.

"Where've you been?" Mum asked, as Rachel walked in. "Dinner's nearly ... have you been crying?"

The phone rang. Rachel only picked it up to avoid answering her mother.

"Rachel? It's me." Dad sounded almost as upset as she was. "I've made a bit of a mess of things," he told her, his voice betraying an unfamiliar humility. "I'm sorry I haven't been in touch for a while."

"I've missed you," Rachel replied, realizing as she said this that it was true. Her father had many faults, but he was her father. She needed to know that he was around.

"I haven't got a place where you can stay yet," he told her. "I'm in a crummy bedsit. I don't want you to see it. But I thought maybe we could meet up tomorrow or Sunday, go for a walk, like old times."

"I'd like that," Rachel said.

Over dinner, Mum asked about the conversation, but Rachel didn't say much. From what Dad had said, it sounded like he might be at fault in the breakup with Clarissa. Rachel didn't want to tell Mum that. Mum didn't press the matter. She was preoccupied with all the extra school governors' meetings she had to go to. The cuts they had to make depressed Mum. She'd even talked about resigning, but didn't want to let the others down. They'd agreed to stay or go together.

Rachel went up to her room. She began to compose a letter to Mike. She wanted him to realize how much she loved him, how much seeing him meant to her, how happy he'd made her. She would sneak it to him in an English lesson next week. No. He would say that was too risky. She would post it.

When she'd finished the letter, Rachel read it back. The

first time she read her own words, Rachel was convinced that Mike would be moved by them. He'd sacrifice his job if necessary, give up anything to be with her. Maybe they would even elope and marry.

Rachel got an envelope, then addressed and stamped it. She put the letter in, but thought twice before sealing it. After a while, she got the letter out and read it again. This time, her words seemed soppy, immature. She imagined Mike marking it the way he marked her English essays, underlining points where she'd repeated herself. Even her handwriting looked young, unformed. If she sent this letter it might give him the excuse he needed to finish with her.

Was he looking for an excuse? Why did she doubt Mike? He'd told her he loved her, that he always would. Rachel believed him. Nevertheless, she put the letter away, in the drawer where she kept her pills. It was time to start a new packet. She'd started taking them on a Thursday and it was now Friday, so she was a day late. But Rachel wasn't having sex at the moment, so it hardly mattered.

When she went to bed that night, Rachel got out the letter and reread it. This time, her words left her cold. All those protestations of love, what did they mean? They sounded like she was trying to convince herself more than she was Mike. You could promise to love someone for ever, but what if you stopped loving them, the way Dad must have stopped loving Mum? What if you couldn't help it? What if what Mike called "romantic" love was only a lie, a convenient fantasy, an excuse for people to get into bed together?

For that was what Rachel wanted now: the wonderful feeling of Mike next to her beneath the sheets, his body pressing against hers, his warmth and softness, the sweet, yet slightly sour smell of his skin. That was what she wanted. And, yes, him moving inside her, their bodies grinding against each other until they both exploded, that too was important. But if she had to choose between the two, Rachel would settle for the holding, the cuddling, the physical certainty that, at that moment, she was wrapped in someone's warm and tender love.

Whatever love was.

The next day, Rachel's father took her for a walk in Woodthorpe Grange Park.

"Remember how I used to bring you here when you were a kid?" he asked.

Rachel said she remembered. She didn't say that she had been here several times recently, with her lover. Dad didn't ask about boyfriends. He was too wrapped up in his own love life.

"What happened?" Rachel asked, as they passed the pitch-and-putt in the May sunshine.

Dad seemed reluctant to tell her. "I made some mistakes," he said.

"And what about Clarissa? Did she make mistakes, too?"

"I suppose so. But not the same kind of mistakes."

Rachel grasped what he was saying. "You've been seeing someone else?"

Dad didn't reply, but Rachel knew her father. That meant "yes".

"Presumably things went wrong, between you and Clarissa?"

"I guess so."

Rachel had so many questions, but didn't know how to ask them. This was, after all, her father. Was Clarissa seeing someone else too? Was her father's affair serious? Why couldn't he open up and tell her?

"I'm supposed to be so good at this," Dad said as they got back to the car. "Talking to people your age. How come when it's my own daughter I can hardly express myself at all?" His eyes pleaded with her.

"It doesn't matter," Rachel said, because that was what she thought he wanted to hear. They hugged.

"I'd hate it," Rachel went on, "if I didn't get to see Phoebe and Rowan any more. I couldn't stand that."

"I'll make sure you see them when I've got access properly sorted out," Dad told her. "It's a bit of a mess right now."

Already, Rachel noticed, Dad was using social worker words like "access". It meant that he and Clarissa weren't going to get back together. Rachel felt a brief surge of triumph. After the way Clarissa had treated her when they last met, she didn't want the woman to be happy. But Rachel loved her half brother and sister. Clarissa would be looking after them. How could Rachel wish hateful things for Phoebe and Rowan's mother?

"How's the revision going?" Dad asked.

"Fine," Rachel lied.

"You know if you want any help, of any kind ..."

"I'll be all right," Rachel said.

Dad dropped her off at the house. "I'll be in touch," he said.

Rachel kissed him on the cheek. Some more of the hairs in his sideburns had turned grey, she noticed.

"Take care, Dad," she said.

Only as he drove off did Rachel realize that he hadn't given her an address or phone number. It would be weeks before she saw him again.

Three

The following Thursday morning's year-seven lesson was not one of Mike's best. The class had spent a couple of weeks working on verse forms. *Haiku* and shape poems had gone really well. They'd moved on to the ballad, which some had coped with better than others. Today's lesson was a kind of summing up. Mike had chosen to finish lightheartedly, with the limerick.

"People often dismiss limericks as a joke," he explained to Judith Howard, as they walked to his classroom. "But they're also a very precise form which requires an understanding of scansion and the ability to tell a story."

It sounded convincing to Mike. Judith nodded politely, implying that she'd heard it all before. She was about to do his final assessment.

Unfortunately, the stories that half the class wanted to tell were smutty ones. Back in the autumn term, this class had been sweet, almost innocent. Now they revelled in jokes about condoms and men who only had one ball. Twice, Mike had to stop children from telling toilet jokes. As the lesson drew to an end, he was running out of reliable girls to read their work to the class. Paul Wilks put his hand up.

"This isn't a silly one, is it, Paul?"

"No, sir. It's about you."

"I'm not sure ..."

But there was an immediate outcry from people wanting

to hear the poem. At the back of the classroom, Judith Howard gave what, for her, passed as an amused smile.

"Go on, then," Mike said, benignly.

The class quietened. Paul read, his voice constantly threatening to burst into laughter:

"There once was a teacher called Steadman,
Who thought he'd died and gone to heaven.
At the end of each day
After school, he'd stay
Screwing Rachel from year eleven."

The class burst into hysterics. Mike felt his face turning red. He could see Judith Howard frowning. The lesson would be over in a minute. Somehow, Mike had to carry it off. He made a calming gesture with his hand, put a fixed smile on his face, and began to speak.

"Now, that was very silly, Paul, wasn't it? But let's ignore the subject matter. It did scan well, although *Steadman* and *heaven* are what we call a half rhyme. The only problem, I thought, came with the fourth line ..." Mike counted out the syllables with his fingers. "As well as being grammatically clumsy, you were one syllable short. Still, good try. Next time, come up with a more sensible topic."

The bell went and Mike dismissed the class. Judith Howard came over. Mike could hardly look at her. The lesson hadn't been that bad. He knew he'd passed his probationary year. But he didn't know what to say if she asked him about Rachel.

"You went a bit close to the edge once or twice there," Judith said, sitting on Mike's desk. Then she smiled. "I'm glad to see that not all your lessons are textbook perfect. It makes the rest of us feel more adequate."

Mike gave a polite smile. This must be a tactful way of

telling him that his lesson stank.

"But you dealt with the smut quite effectively," Judith went on. "Especially that boy at the end. You must never react to such stories. That's how rumours start."

Mike breathed a sigh of relief. She'd heard the gossip, but didn't believe it.

"You've got an interview in Mansfield tomorrow," Judith went on.

"A sixth-form college, yes."

"I don't want to put you off," Judith said, which meant she did, "but you do know nearly half the staff there resigned this year after a new Principal took over? They've got A-level class sizes bigger than ours in year seven."

"No," Mike told her. "I didn't know that."

"Just thought I'd warn you," Mike's Head of department said, as she left. "Interviews don't always give a true picture of a place."

Mike sat alone in his classroom, thinking. Did he really want to work in a sixth-form college? The marking and preparation would leave him even less time for a social life than he had already. He wanted to work at a school with a sixth form. But the jobs weren't coming up. Every week, there were articles in the educational press about how half this year's trainee teachers were unlikely to find any kind of post. Mike was more expensive to employ than they were.

If it weren't for Rachel, Mike's best bet might be to stay at Stonywood. But the atmosphere at the moment was hellish. Not enough teachers had volunteered to take redundancy. Everyone was waiting to find out who would have to go.

At lunchtime, Mike sat in the dining room, at a table reserved for teachers. He liked to have a decent lunch. Now that he was on his own at home, he rarely had the energy to cook dinner. Recently, though, kids seemed to be pointing in his direction. Nearby laughter might be aimed at him. Maybe he was imagining it. At least Rachel didn't eat school lunch. Otherwise, he'd never dare come in here.

Mike sat next to Joyce Jones. She asked how Mike's lesson observation had gone.

"It was OK."

"Judith told me there was a limerick about your love life at the end."

Mike frowned. If Judith had mentioned it to Joyce, did that mean she was taking it more seriously than he'd thought? Or did she regard it as a joke? Joyce gave Mike a quizzical look. She was waiting to see how he'd react. Mike tried to flirt.

"The kid got it wrong, Joyce. He said I'd got the hots for a girl in year eleven. In fact, we both know that I'm planning a passionate affair with you."

Joyce smiled. "In your dreams, sunshine." She paused, then added, "Seriously, people are beginning to worry about Rachel Webster. The play doesn't seem to have done her a lot of good. She's behind in her work, poor attention span, a bit of a burn out, by all accounts. How's she getting on in your lessons?"

"Fine, fine," Mike told her.

It wasn't true, but what else could he say?

"Well, that's something."

Mike worried about Rachel. What if she did mess up her exams? He would be partly responsible.

"Mr Steadman?"

Mike looked up to see the Head at the side of him.

"Come and see me in my office at one, would you?"

"Er, yes. Of course."

Then Mrs Perry was gone.

"What was all that about?" Joyce asked.

"I don't know."

"Maybe she's heard the rumours about you and Rachel Webster and wants to find out if they're true."

Joyce said this in a lighthearted way, but, seeing Mike's reaction, she shut up. Mike couldn't eat. Leaving his food unfinished, he took his tray over to the slops bucket and emptied his plate. Then he retreated to his classroom to think.

The half-hour until one passed unbearably slowly. Mike didn't know what to do. He could try to find Rachel, check if anyone had spoken to her, make sure that their stories matched. But he didn't know where she was. Also, if they were seen it would really give the game away. Mike was meant to be seeing her tonight, but that would be too late. Anyway, Rachel was bound to have denied everything. She was too bright to get caught out. It was himself he ought to be worrying about.

The bell went. Mike didn't have a tutor group, and he had a free period after lunch. The Head could grill him for as long as she wanted to. It occurred to Mike that, as this was a disciplinary matter, he ought to take along his Union rep. However, Mike knew how Sarah Poole felt about teachers who slept with their students. He couldn't face going to her for help.

Mike walked over to the administration block.

"The Head's expecting me," he said to the school secretary.

"I think she's got somebody in with her. Give a quick knock to let her know you're there."

Mike did as he was told. There was no response to his

knock. Standing in the corridor, he felt like a schoolboy, sent to the Head's study for smoking. Two minutes passed slowly. The bell went for the first lesson of the afternoon and Judith Howard left the Head's office, without glancing in Mike's direction. So she had believed the gossip, Mike realized. He didn't hear the buzzer in reception, but the secretary slid open the glass window and spoke to him.

"She'll see you now."

Mike went in to face his sentence.

"Everyone knows," Rachel told Becky, as they walked over to maths.

"Nonsense," Becky said. "The only people who know for sure are me, Mr Hansen and his girlfriend. Everyone else has just heard rumours. Remember that one last year, about Kelly Quick being pregnant? It died away after a while."

"Yes," Rachel said, "after she'd had the abortion."

"That was only a rumour, too."

"What I want to know," Rachel went on, "is where the story started."

"The way I heard it," Becky told her, "was that Steadman was noticed driving you home once too often – after the play was over. I mean, did you think you were invisible?"

"I suppose so," Rachel said. "Yes."

"You'll be all right."

Rachel wasn't convinced. Becky, like most people in their year, was preoccupied with the exams. She didn't have time for gossip. But other people did. At least Rachel had persuaded Mike to see her tonight. They'd talk it over.

The two girls reached the maths block, where, being in

different groups, they separated. Rachel walked into the classroom and took her place next to Carmen.

Kate Duerden leant over. "Loverboy next lesson, eh, Rachel? I'll bet you can't wait."

Suddenly, Rachel snapped. She found herself shouting. "Why don't you grow up, you pathetic bitch? We're not all obsessed with sex, like you!"

Kate reached over, grabbed Rachel by the hair and tried to slam her head against the desk.

"You think you're so special," she shouted, as Rachel struggled, "because you were in a play and you've been screwing a teacher. But you're just ..."

"What's going on here?"

Phil Hansen had walked into the room. By the time he'd strode over to the two girls, Kate had let Rachel go.

"Outside! Both of you!"

Rachel stood in the corridor with Kate Duerden sneering beside her. Rachel had never been in serious trouble before, certainly not for being in some kind of fight. She felt humiliated.

"What was all that about?" Mr Hansen asked. Kate was silent. Mr Hansen turned his gaze on Rachel.

"Well? Was this a completely unprovoked attack?"

"She called me a bitch," Kate blurted out, trying to defend herself.

Rachel tried to explain. "She was spreading nasty gossip about me, sir."

Mr Hansen nodded seriously and turned to Kate. "Is this true?"

Kate stared at the floor. "Some people can't take a joke," she said.

Rachel wasn't sure if this meant that Kate didn't believe

the rumours, or that she was covering up for Rachel. Either way, she was grateful.

"All right, Kate," Mr Hansen said. "Go back inside."

Now Rachel was alone in the corridor with Phil Hansen. He spoke quietly and deliberately. "I'd keep you in detention over break, Rachel, but I wouldn't want to start any more rumours. Remember this: if you react to gossip about you and Mike, people are much more likely to believe it."

"I know," Rachel said. "I'm sorry."

"You've only got a week of school to go. See if you can survive it without getting into any more fights."

"Yes, sir."

Rachel went back into the room, feeling terrible about herself. What would Mike think when he heard?

"This isn't a formal meeting," Mrs Perry said, as Mike sat down. "But it is official. Do I make myself clear?"

"Yes."

He wasn't going to be sacked, Mike realized. He was going to be offered the opportunity to resign. He would never teach another lesson here again.

"Is there anything you want me to know?" Mrs Perry asked.

Mike shook his head. He wasn't going to make any confessions.

"Judith Howard tells me that you have a job interview in Mansfield tomorrow, and that you're very likely to be offered a post."

"The first part's true," Mike said. "I'm not so sure about the second."

"Judith also tells me that were you to be offered a job at this school, you would take it. Is that correct?"

"Yes," Mike told her, hesitantly. "I did say that."

"Very well," Mrs Perry said. "The situation is this. The governors are tonight agreeing a redundancy plan which will allow us to keep your post. I can only offer you a one year contract – but that's all that any school or college is likely to be offering in the current climate. However, our numbers are going up. Your contract will be renewed. And, if Ms Howard's confidence in you is justified, then there's every prospect of promotion before too long."

Mike's head reeled. He'd thought he'd come in for the chop. Instead, he was getting the red carpet. Mrs Perry was offering Mike her hand. He shook it.

"Tell no one of this until it's announced to the staff. You'll get a phone call if the governors' meeting doesn't go the way I expect. But, otherwise, I'll expect you to withdraw from the Mansfield job and show up for work tomorrow."

"Fine," Mike said. "Thanks."

He went to his classroom and sat down. For a few minutes, Mike was elated. But, after a while, he began to wonder whether he'd done the right thing. He was being offered years of being Judith Howard's stooge, helping to put on plays and God-knew-what-else, and for what? The distant prospect of promotion and job security? Why had he accepted? And what on earth would he tell Rachel?

In the last lesson of the afternoon, Mike made year eleven do a past language paper. He didn't make eye contact with Rachel once. Nor did Rachel look at him. When they'd spoken earlier in the week, Rachel had been so desperate that Mike had agreed to pick her up tonight and bring her back to the house. He should tell her that it was off, but didn't dare attempt to have a private conversation with her. There was a funny atmosphere in the class. Kate Duerden, for one, kept staring daggers at him. Mike didn't want to do anything which might make anyone suspicious, especially now that he'd accepted the job.

In the car, Phil told Mike about an incident between Rachel and Kate Duerden.

"What exactly did Rachel say?" Mike asked.

"I didn't hear. All I saw was Kate trying to slam Rachel's head against the table as I walked into the room."

"But Rachel's all right?"

"She was embarrassed, obviously."

Mike was silent for the rest of the journey, hiding how much Rachel's behaviour disturbed him. He dropped the maths teacher off without their discussing the redundancies which were being decided that night. Mike had, after all, been sworn to secrecy. Maybe Phil would keep his job. Maybe Mike would change his mind, go to Mansfield in the morning. He didn't know anything any more. The only thing he knew was that he couldn't see Rachel again until she'd left school. It was too dangerous.

Four

On Friday morning, break was extended by five minutes to allow time for a special staff meeting. The teachers who were being made redundant would have already been told, Mike knew. But the suspense was still unbearable.

"There were two volunteers to take early retirement," the Head explained to the packed room, "but, because of curricular needs, we were only able to release Jim Ford, from Languages. Despite severely cutting part-time hours, we still had to make three redundancies in order to balance the budget. After detailed discussion and consultation, the areas chosen were PE, special needs, and maths. The staff affected are Jan Brice, Carolyn Wharton and Phil Hansen. I make this announcement with the greatest regret. They're all excellent teachers and will get superb references, but there's no way of softening ..."

What the Head had to say next was lost in murmured discussion. People were reaching round to console the sacked teachers. Jan burst into tears. Mike realized that Phil hadn't even come to this meeting. He couldn't face everyone. The two men had drifted apart lately, but he was still Mike's closest friend at the school – his closest friend *anywhere* at the moment, unless you counted Rachel. Mike left the meeting and went to look for him.

Phil was in his classroom, getting out the materials for his next lesson.

"Meeting over?" he asked, as Mike walked in.

Mike shook his head. "Still happening. It's pretty gruesome. I wanted to see you."

"Thanks."

Mike sat on a table next to his friend. "What will you do?"

"Look for another job, I suppose," Phil said. "Do some supply teaching, if I can get it. Tracey's willing to move, but I don't want to make her leave friends and family. She's lived here all her life. I might even quit teaching. They're opening the new Inland Revenue offices soon. I might go for a job there. It'd be boring, but safe. What do they say? The only sure things in life are death and taxes. At least I wouldn't have to take work home every night."

Mike was glad that Phil was being philosophical about it.

"What about you?" Phil asked. "What will you do?"

Mike was confused. "How do you mean?" he asked.

"I presumed ..."

Mike became embarrassed. "They're keeping me on."

Phil looked hurt. "But ... you were only on a temporary contract. And I thought you wanted to leave anyway. The thing with Rachel ..."

Mike shook his head. "I don't know how that's going to work out, but they offered me another year's contract and I couldn't afford to turn it down."

"No," Phil said, bitterly. "I don't suppose you could."

Rachel got home on Friday evening, relieved to have reached the weekend. She had only four more days of school to go. Then it was the exams, for which she was hopelessly unprepared. Already, she was reconciled to retaking maths in the autumn. The rest, she would muddle through on talent, the way she always had. Actresses didn't need great exam results.

"Is your boyfriend back yet?" Mum asked, as they were eating dinner. Mum sometimes made allusions to Rachel's mysterious boyfriend. Making him sound familiar muddied the truth – that Rachel's secret was pushing her and Mum further and further apart.

"Not until after the exams," Rachel said, not looking up from her food.

Last night, Mike had stood her up. It was to have been their first meeting in weeks. She'd waited in the usual place, by the phone box, for ages. Finally, she'd rung him.

"I'm sorry," he said. "I thought you'd realize that it was off, after what happened this afternoon. We can't take the risk."

"Nothing happened, not really," Rachel said, feeling like a schoolgirl, making excuses. "Kate went a bit crazy, that's all."

"We'll talk soon," Mike said. "There are some things I have to work out."

"Don't you have an interview coming up?" Rachel asked.

"I'll tell you about it later," Mike said. "I've got to go."

What did "later" mean? Maybe Rachel could call him this evening.

"Have you got another of those emergency governors' meetings tonight?" she asked Mum.

"No," Mum replied. "They're over for now, thank goodness. We made the decisions last night. I'm afraid that three teachers got some bad news today."

"Who?" Rachel asked.

"I'm not meant to say. But there is one bit of good news I can tell you."

"Do," Rachel said. "It's been a while since I heard any good news."

"That teacher you like, Mr Steadman. It was touch and go, but he's keeping his job."

Rachel nearly choked. "But ..."

"Yes, Judith Howard fought tooth and nail to hang on to him. I don't like that woman much, but you have to say this: she fights for her department."

Rachel put down her fork, feeling like she'd been kicked in the stomach.

"What's wrong?"

Rachel looked at her watch. "I was meant to be meeting Becky five minutes ago. I forgot."

"But you never go out on Friday night. What is this? Revision?"

"Er..." Rachel was too wound up to think of a convincing lie. "She's got a problem she needs to discuss. Boyfriend trouble."

"But what about your dinner?"

"I'm not hungry."

Rachel left the table and went up to her bedroom. She still had her birthday money from her dad. She put twenty pounds into her purse so that she'd have plenty for a taxi. Then she hurried round to Becky's.

Luckily, she was in.

"What is it?" Becky asked, once they were in her bedroom.

Rachel explained. Becky made her talk it through slowly. "And he promised to get a job somewhere else ...?"

"Not exactly promised, but he said we couldn't stay together if he carried on at Stonywood. He was going after lots of jobs. He had an interview coming up at a sixth-form college in Mansfield. I don't understand. We were talking about moving in together."

"But does it mean he's finished with you?"

"I don't know," Rachel said. "I feel betrayed. If we keep going out, it has to be in secret. I don't know if I could stand any more of that."

"Why not?" Becky said. "It seems to me that secrecy's half of his appeal."

Rachel burst into tears. "You don't understand. You don't even like him."

Becky comforted her. "I like him well enough. He's a good teacher. But I think that he's too old for you. Still, it's what you think that matters. Do you want to phone him from here?"

Becky had a phone in her room. Rachel thought about it. "No. I just want to go round there. Call me a taxi, would you?"

Becky did it. "You look lousy," she told Rachel. "Go round there looking like that and he'll forget why he fancied you in the first place."

Reluctantly, Rachel made herself up. It was too late to do anything about her clothes – a shapeless T-shirt and grubby jeans. She couldn't borrow anything from Becky, who was two sizes bigger. She felt barely presentable by the time the taxi arrived.

It was odd, making the familiar journey to Mike's without him in the car. Rachel didn't know what she'd do if he wasn't home. As she got out of the car, though, Rachel saw that there was a window open in the terraced house. She could hear music. Rachel paid the taxi driver and knocked on the door.

Bob Marley was on the hi-fi. Mike only played him when

he was in a really good mood. What if he had company? But, Phil apart, Mike had no real friends in Nottingham. Unless... The door opened.

"Rachel! What are you ...?"

"I needed to see you."

Rachel walked in. The remains of a takeaway was on the TV table, along with an open bottle of Pilsner Urquell, an expensive beer which Mike rarely treated himself to.

"Celebrating your new job?" Rachel asked, pointedly.

Mike was flustered. "How did you ...?"

"My mum's a school governor, remember?"

Instead of kissing her, holding her, Mike began to explain. Rachel didn't really listen. There was some stuff about how hard it was to get work at the moment, then a bit more about how he was talked into it, as though this wasn't what he wanted at all. This had been the hardest decision of his life, he said.

"It doesn't mean we're finished, Rachel. It just means that we have to be discreet for a while longer."

"How much longer?" Rachel asked. "A month? A year? Two years?"

"We can see each other," Mike assured her. "But we'll have to keep it quiet until, say ... Christmas."

"I don't want to keep it quiet," Rachel told him. "I love you. I want to shout it to the world. I want to be seen out with you. I don't want to be treated like some bit on the side."

"It's not like that," Mike said.

He looked tired and flustered. There was something of a teacher's impatience in his voice.

"Isn't it?" Rachel argued. "You told me that you'd take any job, no matter how bad, so that we could be together.

Instead, you're staying at the one place where you can't be seen going out with me! I can't stand it. I can't stand it!"

Mike came over and held her. Rachel began to hit him. He held her tightly. She continued hitting him, but began to cry. Then the hitting turned into holding, and the crying into kissing. Rachel hated herself for wanting him so much.

Before long, they were naked on the sofa, grinding desperately against each other. It wasn't like before. It was pleasurable, but it wasn't making love, Rachel realized. It was sex. Afterwards, instead of feeling full, Rachel felt hollow. On the hi-fi, Bob Marley sang a song about running away.

A few minutes later, Mike called her a taxi, and Rachel went home.

Five

Year eleven were demob happy. It was their last afternoon at Stonywood and the place was chaotic. Already, the fire alarm had been set off three times. Mike tried to return final pieces of work and give some last minute exam advice, but no one was really listening. There was a craze going round for writing on the backs of shirts. After all, none of them would ever wear school shirts again, would they? They were allowed to wear what they wanted when taking the exams.

Mike moved from student to student, checking whether they had any problems, asking what they were doing next year. Nick Cowan intended to do English Literature A-level, along with drama and communication studies.

"What about you, Becky?" he asked, as she came over to get Nick to write on her shirt. "What are you going to do next?"

Becky gave him a funny look. She was the only one in the class who knew about him and Rachel. Not that Mike was sure there was a him and Rachel any more. She hadn't called since she showed up at his house the Friday before. Becky probably knew that too.

"I'm going to get married," Becky said. "Have kids."

"Aren't you a bit ..."

"Young?" Becky filled in for him. "In case you hadn't noticed, teenagers grow up more quickly these days. I want to have a family while I'm young, then have a career when

I'm ready. I don't want to be like my mum. She gave up work at thirty and never got back in."

Mike thought that Becky was mad, but knew better than to tell her so. Becky held out one of the few unmarked corners of her shirt.

"Want to leave a message, sir? Something for me to remember you by?"

Mike looked at the scrawled shirt. The girls' messages were mostly sentimental, the boys' mainly lewd. He recognized Nick's writing: *simply the best*, he'd written, *love from Nick*. Mike remembered Rachel telling him that Nick used to have a thing for Becky. The boy had good taste. What to write? *Good luck*, he put, *Mike Steadman*. Becky turned away and was replaced by Rachel.

"We were wrong," Kate Duerden called out. "It isn't Rachel he's after, it's Becky. Look, he's written on her boobs!"

While Becky demonstrated that this wasn't true, Mike watched Nick write a tender message on Rachel's back. When he'd finished, she turned round and smiled at Mike.

"Want to write something, sir?"

Mike thought for a moment. Nick gave him a funny look. Other kids in the class were paying attention. "Better not," he said.

His students started drifting away ten minutes before the break-time bell. Mike did nothing to stop them. What would be the point? He'd done all he could. The rest was up to them. Rachel was one of the first to go. He watched her leave, a comic book figure with her back covered in doodles. From behind, her new, short haircut made her look boyish. She seemed so young. Yet, six days ago, they'd been ... they'd been ...

It was over, Mike realized, as he sat in the classroom, alone, waiting for the bell. It couldn't go on. He wouldn't tell Rachel yet. It wouldn't be fair to upset her during the exams. But he had to let her go. It would be easier, now that they no longer saw each other every day.

Maybe he had always known that it would end like this. They'd been mad to go with each other, but the madness – the risks, the near misses – had been part of what made it so exciting. They could never capture that again. And the other stuff, all the things they had in common, the talk about living together, they were never really real. On that point, as on many others, Phil had been right. Rachel was too young. She had a life to lead before she started making commitments.

Mike had never had to finish with anybody before. When the time came, he would break it to her gently. Maybe Rachel would work it out for herself beforehand. Maybe the two of them would simply let things fizzle out over the summer. If Rachel was mature about it, maybe they'd even manage to remain friends.

Or maybe not.

Six

Three weeks had passed since Rachel finished school. She hadn't seen Mike once in that time. When they'd spoken on the phone, he'd been distant, only asking about her exams. Rachel had spent a lot of the last three weeks trying to decide what to do about him.

After Mike took the job, Rachel had considered chucking him. It would be better to finish with him before he finished with her. She'd worked out that Mike was bound to leave her. He'd made a choice between staying with her and staying at Stonywood. But they were still supposed to be going out with each other. Last time they spoke, ten days ago, she'd suggested that they sneak a weekend away in the summer. Mike said he'd buy tickets for an open air concert by REM in Huddersfield. But that would be after the exams, which, to Rachel, was a never-never land. You could promise anything there.

In the end, she decided, it was all about love, and being brave enough to love, to go for what you wanted and not give in. Mike had said "I love you" at the end of that last phone conversation, and, despite her doubts, she'd said it back. How could you stop loving someone, just like that? Mike loved her, sure he did. But maybe he didn't love her enough. If that was the case, Rachel didn't want to spend months waiting around for him to end it. She was only sixteen. She wasn't going to settle for anything less than total commitment.

Dad sent a card wishing her luck in her exams. There was no address on it, no sign of him getting back together with Clarissa. Rachel missed Phoebe and Rowan, but there were other things to worry about than her father and his other family.

Her period was late.

Rachel went back and read the leaflets she'd been given about the combined pill. They said that if you started late, you should use a condom as well as the pill. At first, she and Mike had used condoms: *belt and braces*, like the nurse at the Safe Sex Centre said. But Mike disliked the things and putting them on got in the way. Rachel knew Mike's sexual history. They were safe. So they'd stopped using them, even that last time, which was when it must have happened.

It was probably a mistake, Rachel kept telling herself. What was a day or two? Anyway, she had other things to worry about. The exams had begun and, every day, Rachel panicked. Her head didn't seem capable of holding any but the most basic facts. English was OK, and art. The rest – even history, one of her best subjects – were a nightmare. Rachel needed four good GCSEs to get into an A-level course. She'd be lucky to get two.

The final exam was English Literature. This ought to be Rachel's best subject. She knew she'd done well on the coursework, which was worth thirty per cent. In the exam, however, her mind went blank. Mike was one of the teachers in the Sports hall, invigilating. Pale shafts of sunlight streaked across the huge space. Mike walked around it, now and then pausing to answer a query, or escort someone to the toilet. Rachel tried not to look at him, or his shadow. She didn't want Mike to come over and see that her answer paper was blank.

During exams, the hall was unnaturally quiet. The only sounds were the scratching of pens and the turning of paper. In the distance you could sometimes hear workmen having a joke, or moving some bricks where they were extending the music block. If it got too noisy, one of the teachers went out to have a word.

Eventually, Rachel managed to write a reasonable piece about two poems from the anthology, Wendy Cope's "Message" and Liz Lochhead's "Fin". She had to turn them into a conversation between two lovers. Rachel had her couple breaking up. Then she moved on to the *Romeo and Juliet* questions. These should be easy for her, but it didn't work that way. She knew the play too well. One question asked her to write Juliet's secret journal for the night of her wedding. Rachel had already messed up an assignment like that for Mike. She chose to write a formal essay: "*All are punished.* Discuss how far the Prince's words apply to the main characters in the play."

Rachel tried to make notes on the question. But the last answer had taken it out of her. She couldn't do it. Her mind kept going over her own life instead. Rachel's going with Mike broke as many taboos as Juliet going with Romeo. Yet, who was being punished? Mike had been given a job. Rachel, meanwhile, was screwing up her exams and might be pregnant. Why was she the one who had to suffer? Was she the one who'd done something wrong?

"Rachel? Are you all right? Rachel?"

She looked up to see Ms Howard.

"Rachel, you're crying." The teacher offered her a tissue, which Rachel used. She spent the rest of the exam staring at the paper, not writing a single word.

"How did it go?" Mum asked, when she got in from work.

Rachel was on the sofa in the living room, watching *Home and Away*. She had the phone off the hook, and hadn't answered the door when Becky came round, after the exam. She had nothing to say to anybody.

Mum repeated the question. Reluctantly, Rachel answered her. "Lousy. I failed."

"But it was English Literature, wasn't it? I thought that was your best subject."

"It used to be."

Rachel burst into tears. Mum sat down next to Rachel on the sofa and put an arm around her, holding her until she stopped.

"Isn't it about time you told me what's going on?"

Rachel didn't answer. She wanted so much to tell her mum. There was no one she could go to. All of her friends were celebrating the end of the exams. She couldn't bring them down. But Rachel felt like she had nothing to celebrate.

"Mr Steadman was so sure that you'd do well, Rachel," Mum said. "What happened?"

Hearing Mike's name mentioned, Rachel started crying again. Mum held her tightly, loving her warmly, unconditionally, the way a mother was supposed to.

"There, there. There, there."

Rachel pressed her head against her mother's chest.

"You don't have to explain if you don't want to," Mum said. "You're entitled to have secrets. But I'm here to help if I can."

Rachel closed her eyes. It seemed like the ground had given way beneath her and she could feel herself falling. There was only Mum between her and oblivion.

"What is it, Rachel? Are you feeling ill?"

Rachel lifted her head from her mother's chest. "Not ill, no. I think I'm pregnant."

Mum gulped and Rachel cried some more. When she'd stopped, Mum said, "I thought you were on the pill."

"I am. But I'm overdue."

"How long?"

"Coming up to a week."

Mum reassured Rachel and talked about practicalities. She'd be able to take a test tomorrow. When Rachel was calmer, Mum asked another question.

"How did it happen? I thought the boy you were seeing was away."

"He's not away. We just agreed not to see each other for a while."

"Because of the exams?"

"Sort of," Rachel said, evasively. "I'm not even sure if we're going out with each other any more. It's complicated."

"But you're in love with him?" Mum asked.

"I thought I was. I don't know any more."

"And he loves you?"

Rachel didn't know the answer to that any more either. "He says he does. But I don't know what he'd do if I was pregnant."

"He'd be responsible," Mum said. "That's the risk you take when you have sex with somebody. He'd have to support whatever you wanted to do. Do you think this boy is mature enough to do that?"

"He's not a boy," Rachel blurted out. "He's a man."

Mum's voice became stern. "Who?"

Seven

By Friday afternoon Mike was more than ready for the weekend. At least the worst was behind him. The exams were over. Next week, instead of invigilation, he had four extra free periods where his year-eleven lessons used to be. He could relax a little, then spend some time preparing materials for next year.

And Rachel was gone at last. Mike had, of course, been worried when he saw her burst into tears in the exam yesterday. He'd tried to ring her as soon as he got home, but the phone was engaged. However, his main feeling was one of relief. She wasn't a pupil here any more. He'd got away with it.

Would Mike see Rachel again? He had to. The summer holidays were only a few weeks away. They hadn't slept together for nearly a month. He wanted her badly. Sex was a big part of their relationship. He and Rachel might not have a future together, but hopefully they could enjoy a few more weeks, before coming to a mature, mutual decision to split up.

It was his free period. Mike sat in the staffroom, alone, marking year-nine books. To his surprise, Sarah Poole came in, looking as tired as he felt. Mike thought she normally taught at this time.

"What've you been up to, Mike?" she said.

"Pardon?"

"I've just been summoned out of a lesson by the Head," Sarah said, in her most excitable voice. "She said that she wants to see you, with me, now."

"Why?"

"I was hoping you'd tell me that."

This can't be happening, Mike thought. *Not now*. It was too cruel. His brain wouldn't take anything in. All he could come up with was: deny, deny.

"I really don't know ..."

"Then you'd better think as we walk over there," Sarah said. "The Head told me she's brought in the Chair of Governors. That means it's serious."

The governors. Rachel's mother, Mike remembered, was a school governor.

"Have you hit a kid recently?" Sarah asked, as they walked over to the administration block.

"I've never hit a kid in my life," Mike told her, indignantly.

"You'd be one of the few, then," Sarah said. "That's what this kind of call is usually about. You haven't really been screwing Rachel Webster, have you?"

"Of course not," Mike said.

But what else could it be? Sarah kept chattering away. "Good. I did hear the stories going round. You always get them with young, single teachers. They can't be making you redundant, can they?"

"I don't know."

"All right," Sarah said. "Try not to worry. This is probably the Head coming in all heavy-handed over something trivial. Let me do the talking." She knocked on the door of the Head's study.

The door was opened by a middle-aged man who Mike

recognized: the Area Education Officer. Sitting next to the Head was an unfamiliar woman. She must be the Chair of Governors.

"Do you know why you're here?" Mrs Perry asked, gesturing Mike and Sarah to sit down. Mike shook his head.

"We have no idea," Sarah said.

"Really?" Mrs Perry said, her tone not quite sarcastic. "That surprises me."

She turned to the chair of governors. "Mrs Newman, would you like to ...?"

The woman nodded. She was very ordinary-looking, Mike thought. Far too motherly to be a threat. But when Mrs Newman spoke, her voice was that of a magistrate. "I had a phone call from a parent last night, Mr Steadman: Mrs Webster. You teach her daughter, Rachel."

"Yes, I do."

So Rachel's mum had figured something out. But Rachel would have denied it. Mike would be able to ride this storm. If only ...

"Mrs Webster says that you have been having a sexual relationship with Rachel for several months."

Mike's mouth suddenly became very dry. He tried to say, "I don't know where she got that idea from," but it came out as a series of coughs. Sitting next to him, Sarah spoke. "That's an extremely serious allegation, Mrs Newman. I must ask if you have any evidence to back it up."

Mrs Newman gave Sarah a supercilious look. "We have only the girl's word for it, Ms Poole."

"Girls her age are notorious fantasists."

"I agree. However, this one also appears to be pregnant."

Mike gulped. They'd been careful. How could ...

"Do you have anything to say, Mr Steadman?"

"I ... I ..."

"I advise Mr Steadman not to say anything," Sarah told them.

They all waited a few moments to see if he spoke anyway. Mike stared at the carpet, trying to take in what he'd heard. Rachel was having his baby. It changed everything. He had to see her.

"In that case," Mrs Perry said, "I have to tell you, Mr Steadman, that I am formally suspending you from all your duties at this school until such a time as the truth of these allegations is settled. I suggest that you seek immediate legal advice."

Sarah stood up to go, gently lifting Mike by the arm. But the Area Education Officer had something to add. "I should warn you," he said, "that if it transpires that intercourse did take place at a time when the girl in question was under age, the school will be bound to inform the police."

"Anything else?" Sarah said.

All three of them shook their heads, like hanging judges pronouncing sentence.

Sarah didn't speak until she and Mike were out of the building.

"I'll get one of the Union full-timers to call you tonight," she said.

"I'm ... I ..."

"Don't tell me anything," Sarah said. "I don't want to hear about it. Get your story sorted out. I'll give you one piece of free advice."

"What?"

"You'd better make sure Rachel says that nothing happened until she was sixteen. Because if you were having sex with her when she was under age, the police might not bother prosecuting you, but the Department of Education will do something worse. They'll put you on list 99 – the list of banned teachers. If that happens, you'll never work in an educational establishment again.''

Mike got into his car and watched Sarah walk away. The June sun was shining, mocking his misery. Mike waited until Sarah was out of sight before allowing his head to slump against the steering wheel. Why hadn't Rachel called him? Why had she told her mother that she was pregnant, but not him? It could only mean that she had already made a decision, one that he wasn't part of.

Nothing was any good. Mike felt numb, annihilated. He couldn't even cry.

"If I were you ..." Becky said.

"But you're not me," Rachel told her. "You and Gary really want children. I don't know if I do. Certainly not for years. And I don't want to bring a child up on my own, like Mum had to.''

"What does Mr Steadman want?''

"I don't know what Mike wants. I don't even know if I want *him* any more, never mind his baby ...''

The telephone rang.

"Can you answer it?'' Rachel said to Becky.

Becky did as she was asked. Rachel put her head in her hands, remembering all the bad things she'd said about girls at school who'd had abortions. A minute later, Becky came back upstairs.

"It's him: Mr Steadman. He sounds pretty cut up.''

"Tell him I can't speak to him now. Tell him not to call me.''

"Are you sure that's what you want?''

Rachel didn't have to think about it. "I'm sure."

As Becky left the room, Rachel felt a familiar ache. She had made a decision and her body had begun to relax. Why couldn't this have happened yesterday?

"He asked me to get you to call him," Becky told Rachel. "In fact, he begged. He said he'd been suspended from school. He wanted to know if you were definitely pregnant."

Rachel nodded. She wasn't really listening.

"So, are you ready to go the clinic?" Becky asked.

"I don't think I need to," Rachel told her. "I think I need to go to the bathroom. My period's started."

When Rachel came back, she and Becky hugged. Rachel was relieved, but she didn't feel like celebrating.

"What are you going to do?" Becky asked.

Rachel felt tired, and defeated. She'd thought that she was carrying part of Mike inside her and had decided not to let it go on. She hadn't taken his feelings into account, because she wasn't sure how much she trusted him. Now she was bleeding, but everything had changed. She couldn't turn back the clock twenty-four hours. Mike was finished at Stonywood. Was he finished with her, too?

"What are you going to do?" Becky repeated.

Rachel answered with a grim smile. "I wish I knew."

Eight

"I'm not pregnant," Rachel told Mum the minute she came in from work. "My period came."

"I'm so relieved!" Mum hugged her. "I couldn't bear the thought that you might fall into the same trap as I did. Have you spoken to him? Pippa Newman rang me at work. She told me ..."

"I know," Rachel said. "Mike rang up."

Mum looked concerned again.

"I didn't talk to him," Rachel said. "But I will. Later. When I'm ready."

She didn't tell Mum that she'd decided to finish with him because she hadn't made any final decision. What if Mike succeeded in making her change her mind?

Over dinner, the expected interrogation began.

"How old were you when you first slept with him?" Mum asked.

"Why, does it matter?"

"It matters a great deal," Mum said. "If you were under age, the police will be informed. I doubt very much that he'd ever be able to teach again."

"Would you like that?" Rachel asked.

Was Mum really so bitter?

"Yes. I would. I don't think that he should be able to get into a position where he can get up to the same tricks. Do you?"

"It wasn't like that," Rachel said.

"How do you mean?"

"It wasn't like he set out to seduce me," Rachel explained. "If anything, it was the other way round. I wanted him. I made the moves. He'd never have done anything if I hadn't encouraged him to."

"Why should that make a difference?" Mum argued. "He's still a teacher. He's there in place of a parent. Adolescent girls aren't always responsible for their own actions, but he ought to be."

"Oh, come on," Rachel said. "Things like this have always happened and always will. It's nature."

Mum shook her head, then said, wearily, "You sound like your father."

"Why?" Rachel said. "Did he have an affair with one of his teachers?"

"No," Mum told her, in a sad voice. "His students."

"What?"

At first, Rachel thought Mum was joking.

"How do you think he met Clarissa?" Mum asked, patiently.

"Why haven't you told me this before?" Rachel wanted to know.

Mum's voice tried to contain its anger. "Because it's humiliating for a twenty-six-year-old woman to lose her husband to a nineteen-year-old girl."

Rachel ignored this jibe. "I thought that he met Clarissa after he split up with you?"

"He did. This was a different one. I doubt that she was the first, either. And Clarissa certainly wasn't the last."

"She was one of his students?"

Mum nodded. "He couldn't keep his hands off them,

Rachel. Some men are like that. Do you know how many lives he's messed up? Do you understand why I'm so angry about you and this, this Mike Steadman?"

"Yes."

They were silent for a long time. Rachel was shocked. She should have known about her father, she realized. It had been staring her in the face all along. But he was her father and she wouldn't allow herself to think that way about him. She couldn't imagine a girl in her teens wanting to, wanting to ... It disgusted her.

But Mike wasn't like that. Mike and her were real. Once. Part of her still wanted to be with him, this minute, to hold him, to tell him that everything would still be all right. Rachel made a decision.

"I had no idea about Dad," she said. "But you're wrong about me being under age. Mike and I waited until after the Oasis concert, until the day of my sixteenth birthday. He didn't break the law."

Mum gave Rachel a long, hard look. She couldn't tell if her daughter was lying or not. But she could tell that she wouldn't change her mind.

"Then he's more devious than I thought," Mum said, finally.

"He's not devious at all," Rachel said. "We were in love."

"*Love*," Mum said. "I thought I loved your father once. I haven't used that word to another man since. You have to be careful when you say 'love'. It's such a powerful word, and it's used in so many lies ..."

This was the time, Rachel saw, for her to hug her mother, to tell her that she loved her. But there was something else she had to do first.

"I need to go for a walk," she told Mum, "think about a few things."

"I understand," Mum said. "It must have been a shock about your father. I'm sorry I told you that way."

"It's all right," Rachel told her. "I had to find out sometime."

It was a balmy late afternoon. Children were playing in the streets. As Rachel walked to the phone box, she thought about Phoebe and Rowan. She thought about the life that might have been inside her. Then she thought about what she would say to Mike. He needed to know that she wasn't pregnant and that she'd said she hadn't slept with him until her birthday. He was off the hook. Then he needed to know that she didn't want to see him any more.

Was it really what she wanted? She'd told Becky that Mike didn't love her enough. Was that true? Rachel didn't know. Anyway, things had changed. Rachel and Mike no longer needed to keep their relationship secret. They could see each other as much as they liked. They were both free adults.

Suppose, though, that it was always the secrecy which made Mike so exciting? Somehow, hearing about her father made Rachel see things in a different light. What was once special now seemed sordid. Perhaps one day she'd be able to look back at her first love with affection. Perhaps. But not now. Lifting up the phone, preparing the words she'd use to finish with him, Rachel felt no guilt. Mike was a teacher. He knew what he was getting into. He ought to have been more responsible. He ought to have known better.

For the last time, she dialled his number.

Epilogue

The college was so desperate for staff that they didn't question Mike's minimal reference from Stonywood. In the end, because he'd done nothing illegal, the school hadn't sacked him. They had, however, failed to renew his contract, which was only to be expected. As he'd said at his interview here: "I couldn't expect to stay on, with people being made redundant. And, anyway, I wanted more experience. I have a strong urge to teach sixth form."

The hours were worse than at Stonywood, the staff more disillusioned. The pay was lousy, too. You didn't even get a lunch hour. But at least Mike had a job, unlike Phil. Mike enjoyed teaching too much to give it up.

Mike had excellent qualifications. He would worm his way into favour here, getting a good reference for when he was ready to go. He enjoyed teaching A-level, too. The kids weren't as bright as he'd hoped, but there were no discipline problems. You had more freedom than you got in an eleven-to-sixteen school. And, if it didn't work out, he could always register for a PhD. Mike was not yet twenty-four years old. He could still be a university lecturer by the time he was thirty.

A shy seventeen-year-old was nervously reading out a presentation about Shakespeare's portrayal of Cleopatra. These days, Mike got the kids to do a lot of what should have been his work. He was always looking for ways to save time on preparation and marking. He'd tell them to mark each other's essays if he thought he could get away with it.

As the boy talked awkwardly about the Queen of the Nile's sexuality, Mike found himself thinking about Rachel. What was she doing now? He hadn't seen her since the last exam, hadn't spoken to her since she'd phoned to finish with him. He didn't even know her results.

"Is Anthony the love of Cleopatra's life?" the boy asked. "Or a politically convenient pawn for her to manipulate? Shakespeare clearly comes down on the side of ..."

Mike still missed Rachel. When she finished with him, he'd been too depressed to do much about it. He'd drafted a hundred letters, but never posted one. What was the point? On the phone, she'd told him that he didn't love her enough – she'd realized that when he agreed to stay at Stonywood. He'd started to explain that her being pregnant changed everything, that he'd give up teaching, marry her, whatever ... but she'd interrupted, telling him that she wasn't pregnant, only late. Then she told him that she'd lied about when they first slept together.

Mike had begun to thank her. He'd told her how much he loved her, but it came out wrong. Mike could hear the sound of his own voice. He sounded like a worm, pathetically grateful after being let off the hook. He'd stopped speaking.

"I'll never forget you," Rachel whispered, then hung up the phone.

Was Rachel the love of Mike's life, he wondered? He no longer even knew if he believed in love. It was a complicated thing, he'd decided, to do with self-interest, and seeing yourself reflected back through a flattering mirror. He'd had his heart broken three times now and had learnt a lesson or two about love. Best not to take it too seriously, but enjoy it where you could.

Mike let his eyes rove around the small classroom. There were twenty-three students, far too many for any worthwhile discussion. However, this was the only education on offer, and they were lapping it up. Mike's gaze settled on an intense but really rather attractive girl who was sitting near the front.

"Thank you, Peter. Has anyone got anything to add to Peter's comments? No? All right, then. Peter, leave that with me. Justine, I'd like you to do the next presentation, please. If you wouldn't mind staying behind for a minute, we can discuss what's required. Now, I think we'll break early..."

There were so many students that it was hard for Mike to remember their names. Some, however, stood out. When they were alone, Justine brushed the hair back from her face and gave Mike a winning smile. Mike sat in the chair next to hers.

"Did you follow all my comments on your essay?" he asked, in a warm voice.

"Yes, sir. I was very ... flattered."

Mike put on his easiest manner. "It was a very good first essay, Justine. And, please, don't call me 'sir'. You're not in school now. Call me Mike."

"OK," she said, softly. "Mike."

"Now, about this presentation."

Mike pulled out a copy of the book and, in order to look at it, Justine moved closer to him. Her shoulder pressed against his arm. Mike let it rest there.

"I'm a bit nervous," she admitted.

"Don't worry," he assured her. "It's not for two days. You

can go away and think about it. Then, tomorrow, if you'd like some help, come and see me at the end of the day."

"I'll do that," Justine told him.

"Good."

As Mike put the book away, Justine saw the *Elastica* tape sticking out of his bag. He'd brought it in to lend to another student.

"Do you like them?" Justine asked.

"A lot."

"Me as well."

"You've got good taste, Justine."

As the teenage girl left the room, she risked a small, shy glance backwards and was pleased to see Mike still watching. He and Justine exchanged a meaningful smile. Whistling a cheerful tune, Mike strolled down the corridor to his next class. This might be a lousy job, he figured, but it had its compensations.

Rachel's dad's new home was a flat in Carrington. It was part of a huge old house which had once been very grand. But that was back in the days when they had carriages, and horses. Today the traffic going by on the main road made loud, constant noise. It was nothing like the leafy, silent street where Dad used to live.

Rachel hadn't seen her father for weeks and was very nervous. There'd been a couple of phone calls, including one on the day of the GCSE results. Rachel only got pass grades in three subjects: English language, art, and history, which meant that no college would take her to do A-levels. She would have to spend this year retaking the exams she'd failed. In the time left over, Rachel was doing a drama foundation course.

The university hadn't started back yet. Dad should be in. He'd finally let Rachel have his address, but hadn't invited her round. Rachel could see why. The building was shabby. The wood in the window frames was rotten. The place made Stonywood look like The Park by comparison. When she rang the doorbell, Rachel couldn't hear it sound. Nothing here looked like it worked. Then a young woman opened the door and Rachel thought she must have pressed the wrong button.

"I'm sorry," she said, "I'm looking for Eric Webster."

The young woman gave Rachel a suspicious look. She had unwashed blonde hair which was covered by a headscarf. She was also very thin, and her face bore traces of acne.

"I'm his daughter," Rachel added.

"You'd better come in then."

As she opened the door fully, Rachel saw that the girl wasn't that much older than herself. She also saw that she was pregnant. It didn't surprise her.

Dad was in a tiny kitchen, reading the paper. The place was a mess. Paper plates and old milk bottles were balanced on a rusting microwave.

"Rachel!" he said, standing up. "I never ..."

Rachel went over and kissed him. "Happy birthday, Dad."

She gave him the new leather wallet she'd selected in Jessops.

"Thanks. But don't tell Fiona how old I am. You've met Fiona?" The girl smiled shyly at Rachel, then went and stood by her forty-year-old lover. Looking at them, Rachel thought about something Clarissa had told her, a few days before.

"*He's a philanderer, but at least he's an honest one. He gets*

a girl pregnant, he marries her. There were girls before me,
and there were girls after, though I tried not to know. But this
new one, he slipped up. So he did what he thought was the
right thing."

Rachel remembered the look on Clarissa's face during
what she said next. It had been frightening.

"*You know what I'd call the right thing? I'd rip the bitch's*
eyes out!"

Dad kissed Rachel gratefully. "You're quite right. I
needed a new one. Though I don't have as much to put in it
these days."

"About Phoebe and Rowan ..." Rachel said.

Dad immediately looked uncomfortable. "I will arrange
for you to see them," he jumped in. "But there are still
problems with access. Clarissa's been a real ..."

"I've seen Clarissa," Rachel interrupted. "We've made it
up. That's what I wanted to tell you. I'm babysitting for her
once a week. Phoebe and Rowan asked me to give you this."

For a moment, as he opened the packet containing his
new pair of gloves, Rachel thought that her father would
cry. Fiona looked away. She wanted no part of this. She had
her own child to think about. Rachel wondered if Fiona had
dropped out of university, the way Mum had had to, sixteen
and a half years ago.

Rachel didn't feel angry about Fiona, the way she used to
feel angry about Clarissa. Clarissa was always a threat.
Right now, however, it was Fiona who must be feeling
threatened by Rachel. One day, perhaps, they would be
allies. But Fiona had a few things to learn about men before
then.

"So, how's college?" Dad asked, a little later. "Got a
boyfriend yet?"

He didn't know about Mike. Rachel was only just beginning to get over him. Sometimes she wondered if she would ever get over him. She'd been hurt by how little he'd argued when she phoned him that night, how easily he'd let her go.

"No," Rachel said. "Well, sort of. I see a lot of Nick – remember him? – he's doing A-levels there. We go out together sometimes, but he's more of a friend, really."

"A *friend*," Dad said, the old flirtatious glint in his eyes. "Isn't that against human nature? Can men and women ever really be friends when they're also attracted to each other?"

"Of course they can," Rachel said.

"Not in my experience," Dad told her. "They might say they're only friends, but at least one of them is always pretending."

"If you say so," Rachel told him.

She didn't want to have this discussion here, now. If she said what she really thought, there would be too many uncomfortable truths exposed. She tried to turn the conversation around.

"What do you think, Fiona?"

Fiona looked at Rachel's father, as though waiting for permission to speak. "I don't know," she said, finally, feeling the lump in her stomach. "I haven't really thought about it before."

"I have," Rachel said. "I think Dad's mixing up sex and love. Friendship's more important than sex."

"Is this the girl who, only six months ago, was starring in the greatest romance of all time?" Dad said, jokily.

"*Romeo and Juliet* isn't a great romance," Rachel told him. "It isn't about love. It's about an adolescent fantasy of what love is. The thing they call love ends up destroying both of them. It never had a chance of working."

"Ah, the certainty of youth," Dad said. "The trouble with Shakespeare is that you can make his plays mean almost anything." He smiled condescendingly, then added, "You still have a lot to learn."

Rachel and Fiona looked at each other, a flicker of contempt crossing both their faces. Eric Webster laughed uncomfortably, as though he'd told a joke. Neither his girlfriend or daughter joined in.

"I've got to go," Rachel said. "There's someone waiting for me."

Dad showed her out with something resembling relief. They kissed awkwardly at the door, but made no arrangements to meet again.

Nick was waiting in the street.

"Thanks for coming with me," Rachel said. "I really appreciate it."

"Was it awful?"

"Could have been worse."

Rachel stood in the street for a moment, feeling faint. She thought that she was going to cry, but didn't. She had learnt to harden her heart.

"Come on," Nick said. "I'll walk you back to college."

As they turned on to Mansfield Road, Nick put an arm loosely around Rachel's shoulders. She hesitated for a moment, then put an arm around Nick's waist. His grip tightened, and Rachel rested her head on his shoulder for a second before setting off. Then they walked back to where they'd come from: slowly, arm in arm, like young lovers, or old friends.

Afterword

I once worked as a teacher, but this novel wasn't inspired by events at the school where I worked. The spark came when I was eighteen. During my first weeks at university, I fell for a girl on my course. We spent a lot of time together, but she was evasive about her home circumstances. After a while I found out that she was living with her former science teacher, who was at least twice her age. I don't know what happened to them. I didn't realize how common such affairs were until years later, when I went into teaching as a stopgap while I learnt to be a novelist.

I started writing *Love Lessons* quite soon afterwards, but it took nearly ten years to get right. I'd like to thank the friends who read early drafts and offered their advice: Sue, Lynne, Lizzie and Beccy. My editor, Julia Moffatt, helped me see the wood from the trees, and this book is dedicated to her.

Nearly every woman I spoke to while researching the novel knew at least one girl who had slept with a male teacher. There were very few love stories with happy endings. Most of the teachers behaved in a far more manipulative manner than Mike does in *Love Lessons*. Many did it again, and again. Even when they were found out, it rarely affected their careers. By contrast, many of the girls suffered psychological damage. A decade or more later, some were still suffering, particularly in their ability to form relationships.

If you've had, or are having, a relationship with a teacher or lecturer, and are worried by the situation, it might help you to talk with someone. The number for your local Samaritans will be in the phonebook. You might prefer to call Childline on 0800 1111 (Freephone). Both services are completely confidential, and are open twenty-four hours a day.

David Belbin